D0715062

Bury Me Where They Fall

Jonathan Watts

Arkbound

Building futures, Bridging divides

Bury me Where They Fall

By Jonathan Watts
© Jonathan Watts

ISBN: 9781912092734

First published in 2019 by Arkbound Ltd (Publishers)

No part of this publication may be reproduced, stored in a retrieval system, or transmitted, in any form or by any means without the prior permission of the publisher, nor be otherwise circulated in any form of binding or cover other than that in which it is published and without a similar condition being imposed on the subsequent purchaser.

Arkbound is a social enterprise that aims to promote social inclusion, community development and artistic talent. It sponsors publications by disadvantaged authors and covers issues that engage wider social concerns. Arkbound fully embraces sustainability and environmental protection. It endeavours to use material that is renewable, recyclable or sourced from sustainable forest.

Arkbound
Backfields House
Upper York Street
Bristol BS2 8QJ
England

www.arkbound.com

Bury Me Where They Fall

*"You cannot kill mythology.
It goes on, sometimes in a very bad way."*
- Anselm Kiefer

Chapter One

Amiel kept her head high and stared straight ahead with steely eyes. She might be condemned, but she would not let them think she was broken.

Gripping an arm each, the guards led her deeper into the town. Soldiers marched through the streets, among grey-faced civilians. Amiel's eyes narrowed. This wasn't right. Her training complete, she had left the barracks here and travelled further into the Empire. The town then had been thriving, renowned for its sculptures, its trade booming. Now, three years later, something was hanging over the place. Amiel could smell tension in the soldiers, fear in the civilians.

This was a town under siege.

As the thought formed in her mind, Amiel looked around with new eyes. Distracted from her coming punishment, she saw houses boarded up, streets blocked with sandbags and random debris. Communications were slow in an empire of this size, but surely a threat to their frontiers would have been reported?

"What is happening here?" she asked her captors.

"Be quiet," one snapped. The other looked at her, almost apologetic, but said nothing. Amiel did not press them. Ahead, the barracks loomed. It was time.

She expected them to keep her waiting, but as soon as they entered through the arched stone doorway, an aide met them. They were led into a shadowy corridor, small stained-glass windows providing glimpses of the light outside as Amiel walked towards her fate. Still she strode forward, her feet not dragging. She had met everything in life head on; her death would be no different.

They reached the end of the corridor, and the aide tapped on a dark wooden door. A voice from within sent

Amiel back to happier times.

"Enter," ordered her trainer, her mentor; the woman who would order her death. One of the guards opened the door, and motioned Amiel through. They made to follow her, but the woman spoke again. "Just her; you remain outside."

"But-" the guard who had silenced Amiel objected.

The woman cut him off, her tone now acidic. "If she attacks me, I'll be sure to scream so you can come and save me. Now remain outside."

The guard mumbled something, saluted and withdrew. The door clicked softly shut behind him. Amiel didn't look back. The room was as well-lit as it could be, with the day so faint and grey. She almost smiled as she looked at the maps and charts covering every surface, but for the first time since she had left the frontier, the reason for her return began to haunt her.

"Step forward, Amiel."

The young soldier jerked back to the present and looked to the source of the voice. The short, grey hair framing the woman's face was familiar, but Amiel's heart nearly faltered when she saw how her mentor had aged.

The Barracks Commander sat at her desk, letters and parchments spread out before her. Amiel stepped forward and saluted. The silence lengthened.

"I wish it was good to see you again," the Commander said. "How long has it been since you left?"

"Three years, Commander Holheim."

"Of course," she paused. "And since I don't remember including it in your training, it was obviously during those three years you decided orders no longer applied to you."

"That's not what happened," Amiel objected. "I-"

"*Quiet!*" roared the Commander.

Amiel's stomach lurched. In all of her time here, she had never heard Holheim's voice raised. The Commander seemed shocked too.

"I'm... sorry," she said. "Things have been difficult here lately. And it is painful to see you like this. You were one of the best, Amiel. You excelled in training, got recruited into the Tenth Squadron. Guerrilla combat across the Empire, covert operations, the hardest missions for the greatest soldiers."

She shook her head, then turned her gaze back to Amiel.

"And now I see you back here in disgrace. Disobeying orders? What did you think the army would do? Just give you another mission? Let you look after the horses? What?"

"Those orders were wrong," Amiel said softly. "I am not a murderer."

Holheim's chair scraped the stone floor and she walked over to a window, gestured Amiel to join her.

"What do you see out there?"

Amiel looked. She could see the training ground, new recruits hefting practice swords or shooting bows at dummy targets. New recruits, just as she had been once. Their minds were full of fire and the will to defend the Empire, not knowing what that would really involve.

"I see soldiers training."

"Do you? I see men and women from a frontier town of the Empire. The children and grandchildren of the conquered. I see people whose ancestors fought against us, some of them just beyond living memory. Some of them very recently within it. Before we brought this land within the borders of *Theos*, before our soldiers intermarried and mixed enough for them to feel like citizens, before we reached a compromise... *they were the enemy*."

Holheim turned to fix Amiel with her stare again. "The last uprising here was what, ten years ago? Not long at all. You should know. You were here. You were involved. You were the enemy to them then, as well as now. You know how it happens. Some firebrand claiming pure blood and descent from an ancient king gets a group of idiots whipped up against the distant Emperor, promising self-rule and castles for all. And when word gets out about you, you of all people... the question will be, 'if their own army doesn't follow orders, why should we?' By disobeying, going against the law of *Theos*, you've thrown a spark in an old pile of dry wood."

The commander returned to her desk.

"And we have enough fires to put out already. Fortunately, though, I am going to use one of my problems to solve the other."

Amiel looked again at the Commander, thinking back to the strange state of the town. "What is happening here?" she asked. Holheim took a deep breath. "We are under attack."

"By who?" Amiel then noticed the Commander's hand – how hard it was gripping the edge of her desk.

"We *don't know*," Holheim answered, shaking on the last two words. She fought for control, the effort showing in new lines around her eyes, her mouth twitching.

"I'm sorry," she said again. "I haven't slept well since it started. That's when they come. At night. We never see them, only hear them. I hear screams, howling in the darkness. Sometimes it doesn't even sound human."

"And you don't know who they are? Have you not fought back?"

"Three weeks ago, it began. We heard the... sounds at night. It's always the same. We hear them, we see nothing. And in the morning..." the Commander faltered

"What?"

"In the morning, we count how many have disappeared. There are never any dead. No bodies, either ours or theirs. When the light comes, we are... fewer than before. That's it. Tell me, what did you see when you came through the town?"

"This isn't a town anymore," Amiel answered, without hesitation. "It's a military camp."

"Correct. We have set up a perimeter, moved those remaining into these headquarters. By day, we try to go on as normal. Then, at night, we try to defend ourselves. It's not working."

"How many have vanished?"

"Over a hundred, since it began. Soldiers and civilians. No sounds of fighting. Just the screams... and then nothing. I'm trying to keep control but... rumours are starting."

"What rumours?"

"People say *they* are coming from the forest to the West. They're repeating stories they heard long ago. That somethi- some*one* is there, deep within, waiting."

"Ridiculous," Amiel said. "The forest is uninhabited. There is nothing but trees and beyond that, cliffs and the sea."

"Is that so?" Holheim asked. "Then perhaps those who have disappeared are merely playing an extended child's game with me. These... assailants are coming from somewhere, and it's not from the village down the road. What's more, these tales sprung up from several different sources, but share frightening similarities. Someone waiting in the forest. Someone dangerous. With an army. No, I think there is truth behind this, however distorted. I've sent people into the forest. Scouts. Spies. They haven't returned."

"Why are you telling me this?" Amiel frowned.

"Oh, I should think you know," Holheim's hands steepled. "You see, I should execute you for insubordination, but that would serve no purpose. Instead, you are going to solve two problems for me. Firstly, you are going to rid me of these rumours of a warlord amassing an army on our borders, and secondly, you're going to prove that you can follow unsavoury orders and undo the damage you've done to all of us serving the Empire."

Holheim reached for a metal jug, poured herself some water.

"You say you disobeyed your orders because you are not a murderer. Well, Amiel, that is precisely what you are going to become for me. You are going into the forest. You will find whoever is behind these attacks, and you will kill him."

"And if I don't?"

"I said executing you would serve no purpose. I did not say I wouldn't do it."

Amiel nodded, feeling trapped.

"Why did you say 'him'?" she asked. "The rumours all mention the same person, don't they?"

"Decius," Holheim answered. "They all call him Decius. Your hunt begins tomorrow."

Chapter Two

No great weight vanished from Amiel's shoulders as she left the barracks. No sense of rebirth or renewed opportunity lifted her spirit. The town was still haunted around her, the air tense. She remained sceptical about this Decius and his army in the forest. It was more likely a few brigands hiding from the Empire's law.

She tried to smile. It was almost tempting to join them.

Without realising, her feet had taken her left from the barracks, through the town square and to the Church of Saint Janvier. Amiel paused to study the towering building, her hand reaching out to rest on the dark stone wall. She had visited many times in her youth, growing up in the small frontier town. It had never been so busy then as now. Frightened people flitted in and out of the open doors, entering with offerings and leaving empty-handed. Amiel edged around the stream of bodies and entered the church, its familiar atmosphere envelop her. She walked toward the front, where the altar lay under an unaccustomed burden of offerings. Money, food and effigies of Saint Janvier, heaped around the simple stone structure.

She took a seat at the front of the church, searching for calm and watching the altar, knowing the holy remains of the saint himself were buried far beneath her. The saint was known elsewhere, but was by far most popular on this Western frontier, where he was said to have lived. He provided a kind face for their worship, far removed from *Theos*, the grim, distant god who watched all from high above. Scholars further east in the Empire claimed that Saint Janvier was a local pagan god, absorbed and re-purposed when the region was conquered in the name of *Theos* and his Empire. Amiel didn't let their prattling annoy her. Janvier was an important figure in her life, the foundation that her faith and conscience were built on. She knew he had walked the earth as a saint, and done good in the name of *Theos*.

And he was the reason she had disobeyed her orders.

Her mind drifted back to that day, before she threw away her future. Holheim was right. She had been Tenth Squad – expert in dirty warfare. But there was a difference between that and what she had been asked to do. She had looked upon the corpse of their target, dead by her blade, and felt the gaze of his children.

No witnesses. The rebels cannot have any reason to tie this to us. We must be seen as a force for peace.

Amiel walked away, thinking Janvier would have done the same.

But would he? If *Theos* had given the saint an order he didn't like, would he have disobeyed?

She looked now at the statue behind the altar. His stone helm garlanded with lily-of-the-valley, a necklace of stained-glass shards hanging from his chest. Janvier leaned on his great sword and watched over the church. Amiel knew the flowers were replaced when they withered, but the glass shards, cascading down his breastplate in layers of colour, were ancient. The necklace was said to have been placed on the saint himself as he lay dead. Glass shards were an important symbol associated with Janvier. These were said to be the very ones from the windows of his great church, shattered by heretics when the building was stormed and the saint martyred as he prayed.

For the thousandth time Amiel examined the necklace. The shards were all roughly triangular in shape, coming together to form another, larger triangle on his breastplate. Colours sparkled in the light of holy candles: deep crimson, the darkest green, the indigo-blue of the coldest ocean. Silver and golden shards were scattered among them too, and black and white. On some of the shards, Amiel could see the tantalising lines and shapes of what had been illustrated in the original glass, but no one knew what pictures they had painted. Efforts at reconstruction were unthinkable; the necklace was never to be removed from the saint.

Against her chest, Amiel felt her own necklace. Only a single shard, pale green glass, and cheaply made. Nonetheless, she felt that she carried Janvier close to her heart. She sighed, thinking now of her own burden, confronting it head on. Holheim did not expect her to return. That was obvious. The commander had not said how many scouts had vanished while searching for their mystery attacker, but Amiel knew her former commander was thorough and if this had been going on for three weeks, the number would be high. Whatever awaited her in the forest was deadly. So why not desert? Why not secretly double back and head east into the empire, seek a new life? Amiel set her jaw, her eyes still resting on the statue.

Because she was a soldier, and she had new orders.

Chapter Three

Soldiers tried to flank her to the edge of the forest, but Amiel marched ahead of them. She did not speak. She did not look at them. They wore the standard armour of the Empire's infantry, hers was the version modified for the Tenth Squadron. It was more flexible, though just as strong, and engineered to remain silent; no sound of metal against metal would give her away. Her armour was treated to remain dark, not to flash in the light of the moon or stars. At her waist was a long sword, instead of the standard short sword, wielded by hundreds of infantry fighters in close formation to roll over disorganised barbarian armies. It was more suited to outclassing the shorter blades of the lowlifes that the Tenth Squadron usually fought in the grimy corners of the Empire. Amiel wore no helm, just a simple metal circlet rested on her brow, holding back her hair. She had only a small, light shield. It would not stand up to a sustained attack, but it would take one or two blows. That was usually all the time Amiel needed.

Her escort stopped at the edge of the forest. Amiel didn't know if they were expecting anything from her, any speeches or prayers. Two trees bowed inward, forming a natural archway. Between them, a path slithered into the forest, quickly lost amongst the trees. The other soldiers gathered to either side of this gateway, their hands on their weapons as if they expected an attack from within. Amiel paused as something on one of the trunks caught her eye. She leaned in closer, her hand resting on ancient wood. It was the symbol of a glass shard, a slender triangle cut into the bark. Whoever had carved it, she knew their meaning. Her saint walked with her.

She stepped into the trees.

Mist surrounded her, cold tendrils questing across her face as she moved forward. It obscured the way ahead, but Amiel followed the path and did not look to the left or right. It was different and disquieting here, away from the cities she was accustomed to; the filthy, winding stone mazes. She moved as quietly as possible, trying to adjust to her new environment. The sounds of birds, of animals around her, set her nerves crackling. Were they truly animals, or mimicry? Did those sounds belong here, or were they a code? Was she being watched, and word of her progress passed down the line? She would normally have researched the area for weeks, months before even stepping into the forest to search for this Decius. It was one disadvantage among many of being punished with a suicide mission. The wry thought did nothing to amuse her, and Amiel kept on through the mist, her feet digging into years of soft forest rot.

Hours passed, and though stealth slowed her progress, she cut deeper into the woods. Still she heard animal cries, small bodies flitting from tree to tree, the flap of wings. But she saw nothing. She had grown up in the town, of course, and there were no dangerous creatures in the surrounding meadows and smaller woods. However, all the children had known not to venture into the deep green of these trees. Amiel had no idea what could be lurking here, waiting for her. But then she had travelled all over the vast Empire as a soldier, from the steaming swamps where armoured beasts dragged their prey into the green waters and drowned them, to boiling deserts where creatures no bigger than her thumb could bring death with just a sting. She had encountered neither, but found it hard to imagine anything more terrible could await her in this freezing forest, so close to her home. It was best to forget about the animals around her, and focus on her mission.

Decius. Something about the name was familiar. Was it not the name of some ogre or monster, whispered around the fires at night, from old lips to terrified young ears? No, that was not quite right. But it resonated with her somehow, sounding folkloric and ominous in her mind. Amiel dismissed the half-remembered thoughts. Whoever awaited her in the trees was no monster, but a man. If he existed at all. She didn't doubt something was happening to her hometown. The people were terrified and Holheim was not given to foolish overreactions. But a secret warlord hidden in this forest? It seemed like a dream to Amiel.

Something ran across the path behind her. Amiel whirled, her hand instinctively flying to her sword. The scuffling, scrabbling footsteps vanished before she turned, and she could only stare at the empty path behind her, breathing heavily but as quietly as possible. For a long moment, there was silence. There was nothing there.

The animals had fallen silent too.

The bushes rustled behind her again, further into the forest. Something ran across the path again. This time, spidery laughter accompanied the footsteps. She turned, but again too slow to catch it.

Amiel drew her sword, crept forward to where the noise had come from. She could see disturbance on the forest floor, and the broken bushes where her stalker had left the path. But there was silence once more, and everything was still.

Pouring anger onto her fear, Amiel gripped her sword tighter, and faced back down the path. Her voice smashed the stillness.

"I heard you," she snapped. "You're not a very good spy. Most spies I've known have the sense to stay hidden and quiet."

The forest didn't respond, and the silence only lengthened, as if trying to convince Amiel she was talking to the empty trees. She began to walk down the path once more.

"Oh, I wanted you to hear me." The voice behind her was strangely high, and something about it caused a tightening in her jaw. "I wanted you to know you were about to die, and could do nothing to prevent it."

This time when she whirled to face backward, a figure waited for her. It was shrouded in a dark cloak, the hood hiding most of the face. The voice had been unquestionably male. Amiel's stalker was of average height, but painfully thin, something even the billowing cloak could not disguise. In one hand he held a sword, and in the other a knife. His arms seemed a little too long for his body, the limbs too slender, and the lower visible part of his face too narrow

Amiel chuckled, shook her head. "So there is *some* truth to this business after all. Look at you. No wonder you've got them believing there are goblins and ghouls in the forest. How many of you bandits are there?"

The man laughed again, "Oh, that doesn't matter. None of us matter. Only he does. Only Decius."

His voice dropped from the edge of a shriek to a sigh as he spoke the name of his leader. The trees around him rustled, and more men appeared behind him. Their cloaks were hooded too, their faces hidden. Amiel's palm began to sweat as she counted them. There were too many. Sheathing her sword, she turned to run.

"It's no use!" the voice of the thin man had climbed back to its near-screech. *"It's no use to run further in!"*

Amiel heard their footsteps behind her, heard the thin man's screaming breaths and the inhuman noises of the others around him. Like a pack of predators, they chased her. She ran until her chest burned, deeper into the trees and mist, despite knowing they would catch her.

Ahead of her, the trees pressed inward, forming a bottleneck. Far from ideal, but it might buy her enough time to kill one of them; preferably the giggling goblin who led them. Amiel bared her teeth as her hand found her sword once more. *This is what you wanted, wasn't it, Holheim? Decius or death.*

She reached the trees and turned to face them, sword in hand, but they never got close to her.

As the leader sprinted for her, a shadow exploded from the left. It engulfed him and together, shadow and man hurtled off to the right. His scream shook Amiel's teeth in her jaw, but mercifully, after a second, the wail of fear and pain cut off.

There were four other killers, and they stumbled to a halt. Some had their eyes on Amiel, some looked around to either side of the path, peering into the gloom. Their hooded faces were unreadable, but Amiel saw fear in their foolish indecision.

"Where-?" it was all one of them could ask. The shadow struck again: a man strayed too close to the darkness at the tree-line, where their leader had vanished. Something reached out and took him, dragged him into the black. He screamed too, then there was no sound. His torn corpse slammed down into the rot and dirt, thrown from the trees a heartbeat later by something with terrible strength.

The others began to panic. Two ran for Amiel, and one fled back down the path. Beyond the two coming at her, Amiel saw something come from the trees, across the path from where the second man had died. It was tall and slender, and moved like a ghost. It made no sound as it grabbed the fleeing man. Something silver flashed, and he died with a cry of agony. The two before Amiel turned at the sound, and she attacked. Her sword scythed through the back of one man, and she pulled him over backward and tore her blade out as he died. She leapt back into a fighting stance, expecting to face the last. But he stood frozen, staring at the shadow shape.

17

Amiel watched it too, unable to move, trying to make sense of it. In the mist, it had no form. But as it moved closer to the last killer, she saw a tall man, dressed in grey and black. In one hand, he held a sword, a short blade, dripping blood to the forest floor. Step by slow step, he closed the distance between himself and the final man. With a jagged scream, the follower of Decius attacked. The short-sword flashed, and his scream grew higher as blood spurted from his arm. His own weapon fell to the dirt, and he collapsed to his knees. Beyond him, Amiel could see the shadow man standing tall and lean. His sword flashed silver again, glowing even in the sparse light, and where his face should have been, metal flashed as well. He stepped toward the man. At first his victim looked back, his posture defiant, before he deflated utterly and sank into the rot.

"Holy..." there was mortal terror in his voice, and despair. But also, something else. He sounded almost reverent.

The grey warrior reversed his short sword, and plunged it into the man's neck. He ripped it clear and stepped over the fallen body; walked toward Amiel. For the first time, she realised that he was not necessarily her ally, that he might be more dangerous to her than all of the assassins. She fought a mad urge to drop to one knee before the tall man, and instead examined him. His clothing hung close to his lean form. His hair seemed to be black, but none of this mattered to Amiel. She wanted to see his face, but the flashing metal she had seen was a featureless mask. Only his eyes were visible. They were an eerie, pale grey in colour, and although they were directed at Amiel, she felt that they saw only the path behind her. As he reached her, he paused. Knowing his strength, knowing she needed an ally, Amiel spoke first.

"Are you hunting Decius? Who is he?"

"Dec...i...us," the hidden mouth spoke behind the mask. The voice sounded cracked, grating. As if it hadn't been used in too long. "Yes."

Silence fell between them. He was not going to answer the second question. She spoke again.

"I am Amiel, a soldier for the *Theos* Empire." Whoever this was, he clearly had military training. "I am hunting him as well, and could use your strength."

She was wary of this man, as much as she wanted to question him further. He had only spoken two words, but something in his accent was strange to her. She wanted to hear more. He didn't answer her in words, however. He merely nodded once, slowly. But still, she knew she had a deadly new ally.

"Who are you?" she asked, before her fear could stop her. Silence once more. She didn't think he was going to reply, until at last he spoke three more words.

"I... am... Jenvilno."

Chapter Four

Amiel fought to keep up with Jenvilno, the pace making her legs ache as she stumbled along the overgrown path. Where she had moved with stealth, this masked killer marched through the trees without a care. Twigs crunched and snapped beneath his boots, and his eyes stared straight ahead. He did not look to the left or the right; he did not search for hidden enemies. Amiel thought back to the massacre behind them, how he had appeared and disappeared like a wraith. She thought of the butchered body hurled from the trees, and she knew why this man had no fear.

But still, an arrow from the shadows, a knife from ambush. A good soldier prepared for anything. This man didn't even wear armour. His clothes were well-made and fine, but worthless for protection. They blended with the shadows, but what was the point when he walked through the forest like it was his garden? He dressed like an off-duty soldier, or a frontier nobleman out for a hunt. Not a man deep in enemy territory.

And his voice... he had not spoken beyond those final three words. She kept hearing the creaking, grinding voice as it spoke his name, time and again. Something in his accent jarred her ear. It was strange. The rule of *Theos* spread from horizon to horizon, and she had spoken to people in many countries. None of them sounded like this Jenvilno. But something about it took root in the back of her mind, troubled her. Something about it was familiar. Where was he from?

It would come to her, or it wouldn't. She looked now at his sword, belted at his waist. It was a short blade, an infantryman's weapon. Like the standard weapons of her escort to the forest, it was designed to be used in close formation, shoulder to shoulder and paired with a large, heavy shield. Jenvilno carried no shield, and a sword of that length would put him at a severe disadvantage against an opponent armed with a blade like Amiel's, or an axe, or a spear. Amiel's eyes narrowed as she looked at the masked man's back. Someone with his skill could not be dressed and armed this way out of sheer naivety. It was as if he wanted to make fighting more dangerous for himself. Why?

The question was swept away by the sounds of a fight further ahead in the forest. Jenvilno ran ahead, and Amiel followed him into a clearing in the trees. Her soldier's eye took in the scene in seconds, and her step didn't falter. Four more men, dressed in the same hooded robes and dark garb of the others, were attacking a youth at the far end of the clearing. He was quick on his feet, Amiel noted, and well-balanced. But he was armed only with a knife, and his assailants had swords. He ducked and weaved around their blades, but he was already bleeding from a few cuts and Amiel knew that without their help, he would not survive. She pushed herself to run faster, drawing her blade. Six steps took her across the clearing just as Jenvilno reached the first of the men, who managed to turn and raise his sword, but gave a strangled shout as Jenvilno's blade plunged into his gut. The force of the blow almost lifted the dying man from his feet; the masked man ripped his sword free and dropped the body. Amiel drew level with him, and heard a soft word from the hidden mouth.

"Next."

He didn't wait. Like an attacking animal, he surged forward. One of the men moved to meet him, and as they clashed, Amiel sought her own opponent. The youth would have to deal with the third man for now. Amiel's enemy was skilled, but she was a soldier of *Theos.* There was no contest. She swept his blade aside with her small shield, stepped around the sloppy punch she assumed was a shock tactic, and plunged her blade into the billowing robe, feeling it cleave flesh within. She slammed a boot against his chest and dragged her sword free, spinning and raising her shield to block an attack from the final man as he charged in. Behind him, the youth lay on the floor, dead or injured. Amiel had no time to wonder which. The man drew back and slammed three more blows down at her, grinning and babbling as his blade rose and fell. As Amiel leapt back from him, a wiry arm hooked itself around the killer's neck from behind. The youth, much livelier than he had pretended, raised his other hand and rammed his knife deep into the killer's sword-arm. He tore it free, wiping it on his leather coat

"Word of advice. *Never* turn your back on me."

The youth flashed Amiel a grin. His face looked like it hadn't yet felt the need of a razor. The hooded man staggered, screaming incoherent words of pain and dropping his weapon. Amiel surged forward and struck her distracted opponent a killing blow. There was no sound of fighting from behind her. Amiel risked a glance over her shoulder to see Jenvilno's opponent lay dead as well. The masked warrior was moving slowly to join them, pale eyes on the youth. She returned her gaze quickly to him.

"Who are you?" she demanded. "Why were they attacking you? What are you here for?"

"Listen to this!" the youth chuckled. He moved to his left, bent, and swept up a wide-brimmed hat from the forest floor. He ran a hand through unkempt golden hair, and placed the hat on his head with a flourish.

"An interrogation from the soldiers of *Theos*, and not a word of greeting! Perhaps I want to know why you're creeping around this forest in what may or may not be the dead of night." Again, he flashed her that grin. "I honestly can't tell when I'm this deep under the damn trees."

Amiel looked from this boy to Jenvilno, who stood now on her left. Those were men of Decius attacking the youth, and even if he could not be trusted with their mission, she was confident Jenvilno could catch him if he went running off to tell the wrong people.

"We are searching for a man named Decius," she told him. "His stronghold lies deeper in the forest. We are going to kill him."

The boy's smile didn't flicker, "Well, by lucky chance I had very similar business with this fellow Decius as well. I will join you, if you don't mind. It would appear I owe you for your help just there."

"You could have taken them," Amiel told him. "I'm sure if you had played dead and backstabbed them one at a time, they wouldn't have known what was happening."

"Oh, and you're amusing too," the boy shook his head. "My name is Axel Solarius. Might I have the pleasure of yours?"

"My name is Amiel," she told him. "And he is Jenvilno."

"Jenvilno?" Axel asked. The masked warrior abruptly started moving again, marching along the path. "I *was* wondering why you would bring a statue into the forest with you. Does he want us to follow him?"

"If you want to take a different route you are more than welcome," Amiel told him. She began to walk after the masked man, and Axel trotted beside her, keeping up.

"Oh, no. I'm afraid this is the only way to our man Decius," Axel told her. "This is the only path. And across it lie the gates, of course."

A shudder passed through her. Again, something familiar but only half-remembered.

"How many gates?" the question was out before she could wonder why that was the first to occur to her.

"Five, in all," Axel answered, "and each of them

heavily guarded."

"The town nearest this forest is under siege from his men, and they know nothing beyond his name. He's barely more than a rumour. Until I fought men who spoke his name, I didn't believe he existed. The townspeople only hear the shouts, and count their vanished in the morning. How do *you* know so much about him?"

"When you ask in the right places, you find the right answers," Axel told her. "In a fine, well-lit, well-patrolled city like the town you speak of, the taverns are full of laughter and happiness, and talk of how great *Theos* is to bless us so."

"You're old enough to drink?" Amiel was one third curious, two thirds mocking.

"Very amusing. I am nineteen. Now, you go a bit further, you sink a bit lower, and you find the grimy places where no one is afraid to curse *Theos* and his Empire, and maybe you hear rumours of a man with a stronghold deep in a forest, looking to recruit for his new army."

"And is that why you're going?" Amiel's hand was on her blade before she knew it. "You want to enlist?"

"Of course. And I felt the best possible escort was two people who just told me they want to kill him. Do try to think before you speak." Axel cloaked his insult with another grin he probably thought was charming. "He is recruiting. And to do that, you need money. Gold, maybe gems. I feel like he won't miss, say, as much as I can carry."

"So you're..."

"A glorified thief, yes."

"I was not going to say 'glorified'."

"Do you plan to make Decius laugh himself to death?" Axel asked, "I am more than happy to help you through the gates, and past the generals guarding them."

"Generals?" Amiel's heart was racing now. Something was wrong. This was too familiar.

"Yes. Five of his most trusted men. They sit in their gatehouses, and they watch who comes and goes, making sure no one gets through to Decius who shouldn't. We'll need to fight, trick or lie our way past them. I'm very good at the last two. They're each manned by many soldiers, and we are just three."

Here, Axel indicated the masked fighter ahead of them. "Although, I would like to see what he could do with that blade, provided he was on my side. There's something about him that sets my nerves too tight."

Amiel knew what he meant. The way Jenvilno moved was almost *wrong* somehow. Beyond even his explosive speed and frightening strength, the way he held himself and the way he walked were different in some way. But she couldn't waste time puzzling out what was wrong now. Her mind was locked on Axel's words, scrutinising and twisting them: five gates, five generals and a man called Decius.

Why did it feel like a memory?

Chapter Five

Amiel tried to work out what unsettled her about the situation they were in. The forest, the gates, Jenvilno. It was not easy with Axel talking constantly next to her. For some reason the youth thought her interested in his bragging tales of trysts in filthy taverns, and narrow escapes from city watchmen.

"… And, well, how was I supposed to know she was a nobleman's daughter, dancing on a table like that?"

"I can't imagine." Amiel's voice spoke, but she was far away. She stared at the marching man ahead of them. He didn't slow, he didn't tire.

"I might run ahead and join him," Axel said. "Probably better conversation."

"So far I got his name, and a nod to say he's here to kill Decius as well," Amiel told him. "Be my guest."

Axel said nothing for such a long time that she looked at him. He was watching his feet on the uneven forest floor. But he glanced at her whenever he could, his expression strange.

"Yes?"

"You didn't even know for certain he existed before you fought his men."

"What?" Amiel was mystified. Axel was looking right at her now, the slick grin vanished. There was a light in his eyes which made her uncomfortable.

"You said that. And you said at your garrison, they didn't know if this person was real. It was just a name, spoken in fear. Why are you ready to kill him?"

"I don't know what you're talking about."

"Yes, you do. You know how the army works better than I do. Normally they would send scouts, spies to determine what was even going on in this forest. They would bring information back to the leaders, and only then would the machine grind into motion and do something about the man raising an army in their forest. Note that I said *scouts, spies*, plural. You were alone until you met him. Are you even with the army of *Theos,* or are you striking out alone? What sort of soldier are you?"

Amiel sighed, "A disobedient one."

"Please explain."

"I am from the Tenth Division. Or I was. You know that one?"

"Stopping rebellions within the Empire," Axel said, new-found respect in his voice, "guerrilla combat, assassinations."

"It was the last one I objected to," Amiel told him. "A rebel leader in a city far to the east. He was brilliant. Organising riots, disrupting votes in the city with his gangs, killing watchmen. Even our soldiers would be picked off if they weren't too careful. He needed to be neutralised. I was ordered to do it, along with any witnesses." She looked at Axel. "His children. They had hidden behind a tapestry as I crept in. I think he knew we were closing in, and told them to run. But they didn't, and they heard me cut their father down."

"You..." Axel's hand went to the back of his neck, toyed with his hairline uncomfortably. "You didn't know they were there."

Amiel glared, torn between contempt for the unworldly boy and anger at herself. "People who don't notice two pairs of feet poking out from under a wall hanging don't get into elite military squadrons. I knew they were there. I knew what it would do to them."

Axel nodded slowly, silent.

"But I would not kill them too. This was insubordination, they said. Disobeying orders. I was shipped back here for punishment. Before you Axel, you see scout, spy and assassin all in one woman. This mission is my penance. I have to kill Decius. And they don't expect me to come out alive."

"Penance? For refusing to murder children?"

"I'm a soldier," Amiel told him. "I don't get to choose which orders I like. I was wrong."

"You were wrong to kill him in front of his children," Axel snapped, "but only a monster would expect you to murder them as well. It would have marked your soul."

"And what would the liar and the thief know about souls? Do you give to the poor, Axel?"

"I have never harmed a child," Axel told her. "I am not perfect, but I follow my own instincts, not blindly doing what I am told."

"You are not a soldier," Amiel said. "You do not understand. What if, by leaving them as witnesses, I have endangered the other soldiers still stationed in the city?"

"They chose to be soldiers, and they can defend themselves. Children can't."

"And those they protect, the civilians wanting to live in peace, those who suffer violence from the rebels; what about them?"

"Would they want you killing children to preserve their own lives?"

Amiel shook her head in frustration, but remained silent. Axel was naïve, and had never seen a troubled region like that one. It was easy to hold to ideals when the nearest conflict was thousands of miles and several countries away. The Tenth had taught her that morals mostly came in shades of grey, and obeying orders without second-guessing the long-term effects was the only way to keep structure in regions, cities and lives. One moment of poor judgement had brought her here. But never again. She reached for the cheap piece of glass around her neck. Saint Janvier walked with her, and she would remove this Decius and end his terror.

Chapter Six

Toying with the glass, thinking of her saint, it came to her. Axel was talking again, fighting through the uncomfortable silence between them, telling her of the first gate. As he described the general awaiting them, Amiel's hand clenched on the glass, cold fingers trembling.

"The first gate is held by Jotun. A real giant, so they told me," Axel said. "Friendly enough, but still in the pay of Decius."

"A Giant..." Amiel could only breathe the words. "The Giant... and they'll part as friends."

"Excuse me?" Axel frowned.

"It's him. He's finally come." Amiel's fingers released the shard of glass and pointed at their masked companion's back. Her hand shook. "He's Janvier."

"That backwards saint they worship around here?" Axel chuckled. "What makes you say that?"

Amiel pulled mist and air deep into her lungs before she spoke.

"I knew as soon as you mentioned the gates," she told him. "I just couldn't remember. I haven't heard the story since I was small, haven't even thought of it in years. It's not very well-known. Janvier's last quest. It's finally here."

"His last quest?"

"The last pilgrimage of Janvier. The one we were waiting for him to take on. Some said he would return from death to fight evil one final time. Some said he never truly died, and was just waiting for when he was most needed. The noble knight Janvier will fight his way past five gates, defeat the five generals guarding them, and sail up a great river."

"But why?" Axel frowned again, caught between

confusion and annoyance.

"To kill the Mad King, Axel. To rid the world of his evil. Beyond the final gate awaits the Mad King, Deseme. Can't you see? It's happening."

"A lovely story, I'm sure," Axel said. "But his name is Jenvilno, not Janvier."

"But it sounds almost the same," Amiel protested, "like Decius and Deseme."

"Mere coincidence," Axel said. "Decius is no king."

"Then what is he?" Amiel countered, "who is Decius?"

Axel looked uncomfortable, "I... I don't know, Amiel," he admitted. "But it's a myth. Noble knights... saints... quests... how can it be coming true now, hundreds of years later?"

"How can it not?" Amiel asked. "You said yourself; the general who awaits us is a giant. He will be tired of the Mad King and his cruelty. He will let us through, and he and Janvier will part as friends."

"*Jenvilno,*" Axel corrected. "His name is Jenvilno. And he is no knight. He wears no armour, only that mask."

"Saint Janvier swore that no man would see his face on his final quest," Amiel snapped. She quickened her pace, tired of the boy now. She did not fully catch up to Jenvilno, but walked behind him. She looked at the subtle strangeness of his movements, the *otherness* in his frame, and she saw now not wrongness but the divine. This was a saint given flesh; of course his movements were different. At his side, the short sword hung, and she knew now it was the great *Lux*; Janvier's steadfast weapon through all of his journeys, beside him now for the last. She felt the shard of glass against her chest but it seemed hollow now, an inadequate homage to the divine figure now before her. She bowed her head, and vowed that she would help the saint in his final quest.

She knew who Decius was now. He was the Mad King. And together with Janvier, she would end his reign.

***

Hours passed as they walked and, mercifully, Axel remained quiet behind her. Ahead of her Jenvilno marched on, tireless. Eventually, they reached a clearing in the trees, and for the first time in far too long Amiel saw the open sky. Did *Theos* wait beyond the stars? Did he look down on his servant as he marched through the trees? Amiel didn't know about the faceless god, only the saint who walked with her.

To their right, a wide river whispered from the trees, its waters grey against the white mist. It snaked across the clearing, and vanished through a small, arched gate in a stone wall before them. The structure stretched across the clearing, lost among the trees on either side. But Amiel knew it spanned the whole forest, barring their way. The only way through was the great gate-house set to the left of where the river passed through. Huge wooden doors faced them down, set in the ancient stone. Above them was the mighty tower, its crenelated top rising above even the trees.

"The first gate," Amiel murmured. Religious awe gripped her. Around her it was happening. Axel hung back at the edge of the tree-line. Jenvilno glared for only a second at the gate-fort before them, and then once more he began to walk. Amiel made to follow the masked fighter, but a hand on her shoulder stopped her. She turned to Axel, her anger with him forgotten, but impatient now to follow the holy warrior. The youth said nothing. He only pointed to the high crown of the gate tower. She followed his finger and saw silhouettes against the sky, the creeping forms of men.

"They could be archers," he warned. "They could kill us."

"They won't kill us," she told him. "We hold the right of challenge."

She walked away from him now, and followed her saint. She ran to catch up, and together they approached the double door of the fort. Up close, the wood had a red hue, and was held to the stone doorframe with enormous black hinges. Amiel heard the sound of a heavy bar being lifted within, and as they reached the door, it swung open. Shadows greeted them, flickering and twitching with the light of the torches on the wall. Jenvilno stepped into the inner twilight without hesitation, and Amiel followed. Axel was behind her as she looked around herself. She was in a corridor of stone, vanishing into the dark ahead of them as the torches ended. Jenvilno stood motionless, and Amiel was waiting for him to step forward and vanish into the black when a voice called to them from an open door to the left.

"Challengers!" the one word boomed, echoing around the sparsely-lit gatehouse. "Challengers, it has been so long! Come in and join me!"

Amiel led the way now. With Axel and Jenvilno behind her, she followed the voice.

Mythmaking: Part One

The noble knight Janvier will set out to find the Mad King Deseme. He knows the journey will be long, and the path dangerous. But Janvier is brave, and Janvier is strong.

He will dress himself in his armour, bright as a star. He will take up the mighty sword Lux, sharp as the frost. Alone, he will walk into the forest.

At the first gate, he will meet the Giant. The Giant is a mighty general, huge and powerful. But the Giant knows of the evil of King Deseme, and he is tired of it. The Giant will take Janvier to his table, he will give the knight meat and drink, and he will say he wants to help. He will open his gate for Janvier, and the two will part as friends.

Chapter Seven

At the head of a long table sat the biggest man Amiel had ever seen. His face was hidden by a wild growth of black and silver beard, and his great bulk strained against the edge of the table. He was like a bear, or an ogre. His arms were colossal, and Amiel could only guess at the power behind them. Despite his frightening size, his brown eyes were warm, friendly. The surface of the table was covered by an enormous spread of food; steaming platters of meat, fish and vegetables waited to be eaten in vain, for the massive man was the only one seated at the banquet. Chairs were set all along the table, but they all stood empty.

"I am Jotun. Come, sit, eat!" His voice bellowed from within his thick chest, and Amiel found herself warming to the giant. She stepped forward, leading the way again, and took the closest seat to the giant's left. Axel sat opposite her, flashing a quick smile as he reached for the food. Wood scraped against stone beside her, and she turned to see Jenvilno take his seat without words. By now Axel was eating heartily, but Jenvilno touched nothing. The torchlight glinted from his mask, throwing the eye-holes into shadow as he stared at the general. Amiel, too, remained wary. She watched the giant tear a leg from some great roast animal in front of him, but alarm began to twist in her when she caught movement in the shadows.

Behind him, lining the wall to the left and right, stood a group of soldiers. Amiel strained her eyes to see them, but their faces were hidden by the helms they wore, visors down. Only their lower jaws were visible, each mouth set in a grim line. Their armour was dark, and each held a long halberd as they stood to attention behind the general. Amiel tensed, and beside her she knew Jenvilno's hand was not far from his sword. The giant smiled now, and held up a massive hand.

"You are among friends, young lady." His tone was warm still. "I would never kill a guest at dinner, even a challenger. And you are challengers, are you not? You search for Decius?"

Amiel nodded. She glanced quickly at the masked fighter to her right, then looked back to the general. Would he let them through? Jenvilno wasn't as tall as the giant, and his build was far more slender. Slight, even. Could he defeat an opponent of such size? They needed to pass the gate. Amiel knew a fight depended on more than just size, but still she watched the huge man warily.

"Yes, Jotun," she answered. "We invoke the right of challenge. We choose as our champion-"

"Forget that," ordered the giant. "You can pass. I won't fight you." His jovial tone slipped away, and he looked now at Jenvilno, not Amiel.

"You... you'll let us through?" It was happening. Amiel's head swam, though she had not touched any of the wine waiting on the table. Opposite her, Axel had stopped eating, and his wide eyes watched the general now as well. Amiel struggled through the silence in the hall to voice one final word.

"Why?"

"I'm tired of it. Tired of it all. Tired of *him*," Jotun answered. "It must end. The reign of Decius has gone on for too long."

"Who is he?" Amiel's throat was frozen.

"Who is Decius?" Jotun leaned forward, away from the torches behind him. Shadows wrapped his face and gave him the appearance of a bearded demon as he answered.

"He is the Mad King, of course." He let the silence wear on for unbearable seconds before he continued his story. "Decius is the High King of a far-off land. Once he was only a general to the true king, but treachery ran in his blood and he plotted against his master. For years he smiled at the king, with blood and death in his heart. Finally, he murdered the old man, tore him apart and took his throne. At first the people rejoiced. The old king had been a cruel tyrant, and they thought Decius would deliver them into a new age of happiness and light. They were wrong."

Soldiers shifted behind him, weapons scraping on stone and armour as Jotun spoke on.

"Where the old king was cruel, Decius was monstrous. Where the old king thirsted for blood, Decius devoured flesh. If the old king was a tyrant, Decius was an animal, ripping everything to pieces. He is strong, and his mind is ferociously sharp. He turned all of this ability, and all of his malice, on the realm. To be cruel to his people, that was not enough. Decius crippled his entire nation, until it screamed and begged for everything to end. And so it did.

"The people rose up, conquering in each other their fear of the Mad King. They surrounded his palace. They trapped him within its great walls. They meant to send in so many assassins even the evil Decius could not survive, or to burn it down with him inside. But they failed; slaughtered them. He walked untouched from the flames. He cut his way through his own people, laughing the whole time. And he fled. His escape took him far, far from his own realm, to this forest. Here he took refuge and here he waits. In his citadel he waits, and as he waits, he gathers men to him. The lowest of men, the cruellest, those with murder in their hearts and madness in their eyes. He gathers these... creatures around him and he waits only until he has enough, and then he will march out and retake his land."

Here Jotun paused, suddenly unsure.

"Or maybe he will march in some new direction, to another new land that has never heard the name of Decius. Only he knows what he will do next, and only some of the time."

"Why do you fight for him?" Amiel asked.

"I was his bodyguard," Jotun answered. "And then his general, once he crowned himself. It was an honour to serve him. Loyalty is in my blood and my soul. I did my duty for him, and I did it well. But that is over now, it's all over. There has been enough madness. I have been waiting for the right warrior to end this for me, and next to you I see him. You may all pass, and rid the world of Decius."

Jotun stood up. His great hands rested on the wooden table, and his huge shaggy head lowered as he gazed into Amiel's eyes.

"You are finished? It doesn't matter. The feast is over. Comfortable rooms await you higher up in the tower, and tomorrow you will find a boat beyond my tower. It will take you to the next gate."

"Who awaits us there?" Axel spoke for the first time. Jotun's eyes rested now on the boy.

"So, you are part of this too. At the next gate awaits the Great Trickster. Beware his words! Listen not to his lies!" Jotun paused and chuckled. "Though there is little else you will hear from his lips."

He turned again to Amiel.

"No fight today, or tomorrow," he told her. "But I will see you before you depart. I will await you at the river."

"You have our thanks," Amiel told him, beginning to stand. Jotun only smiled and shook his head. Amiel thought she knew what he meant. No gratitude was necessary. She gave him a curt, military bow however, and walked from the room. Axel tried to copy her bow and followed her. Jenvilno forced his chair back and swept past them as he left the room. Amiel caught the quickest gleam from his pale eyes in the torchlight.

Chapter Eight

But Jotun did not appear the next day.

After a night of jagged, familiar dreams, Amiel left her room at dawn to find Jenvilno waiting for her. Now she knew he was the saint born in flesh, it was difficult to behave normally around him. She wanted to kneel, to pay respect, but something in his eyes stopped her. Something in the wall of silence and the hidden face. It seemed wrong. She knew to ask nothing of the saint. She knew her faith required her to follow, and aid him where she could. It was an honour almost beyond her comprehension. But she was torn between a desire to stare at the divine and a need to avert her gaze. She now looked at him, around him, with new eyes. He was tall, but she had seen taller. He was strong in battle, but she had not seen anything inhuman in his speed or skill. She knew more battles awaited them, though, and she knew she would get more chances to see the saint fighting.

With a clatter of his door, Axel joined them. He smiled, settling his hat on his head. Together, the three walked down a spiral staircase, back to the main part of the tower.

The tower in daylight, stripped of its shadow and mystery, was still eerie and the silence set Amiel on edge as she descended to the main corridor. She paused and looked around. The door to the main hall now stood closed, flanked by two of the armoured guards from the previous night. Amiel took the time to examine them in the fresh light. They remained motionless. Their helms and armour were plain, but well kept. It was unadorned, but brutally functional. Heavier than the standard infantry armour of the Empire's soldiers, it reminded her of the cavalry armour she had seen when deployed nearer the flat plains of the eastern Empire. In their hands, they held their long halberds, wrought in dark iron.

"They are guarding the door. Jotun must be in there still," she said to Axel, striding forward to the doors. As she reached them, the soldiers crossed their halberds, mirroring each other and blocking her way.

"What..." Axel managed to choke out, but before he could say more the door opened behind the soldiers and more of them began to appear. These were armed with swords, and they appeared three abreast in the doorway as the two guards returned to their original position. Behind those in the doorway, Amiel could see others waiting. She suspected more lurked in the hall behind, but she fought off her fear. She set her jaw and spoke to one of the foremost soldiers, their identical helmets making it impossible to discern a leader.

"Jotun awaits us," she snapped. "He promised us a boat, and said he would see us off. Where is he? We demand to see him."

She made to move forward, but the soldiers did not part. Helms in place, mouths set, they only waited. Her anger flared, but her voice remained frosty.

"I don't know what game you are playing, but we are done," she told them. She turned to Axel and Jenvilno. "We will find this boat and leave."

She almost cried out when she walked past her two companions. Barring the staircase they had come down were three more of the faceless soldiers. When had they appeared? It didn't matter. She and the other two were leaving. She marched on ahead, following the stone corridor to the far side of the gate-fort. At the end of the corridor was another huge doorway. The doors stood closed, and a bar on their side held it locked. The three of them advanced toward it, but as they closed in on the door, and the next step of their pilgrimage, she heard Axel's quiet voice.

"Amiel?" He was almost masking his fear.

"Yes?" Her voice was sharper than she intended. She turned to find him facing back down the corridor.

"Amiel, they're following us."

She had heard nothing. No footsteps, no hiss of weapons on stone or armour, but the corridor behind them was full of guards now. The silent soldiers with the halberds led the pack; between and behind them stood the swordsmen in perfect file. They filled the corridor, snaking around back to the doorway of the great hall. It was impossible to know their numbers. They were motionless once again. Amiel took three backward steps toward the door, and as one the soldiers moved forward three soundless paces.

"What are they doing?" years of practice and training enabled Amiel to speak with authority, to crush the fear from her words.

"I... I don't know," Axel whimpered. "We should leave. Now."

They moved the last few metres to the door. Behind them, keeping the exact same pace, the soldiers followed. When Amiel reached for the locking bar, they attacked.

Still, they made no noise. The halberd-wielding soldiers stayed in one place, but around them the swordsmen surged. Amiel drew her weapon, and next to her she heard Jenvilno do the same as he dropped into a fighting stance. Amiel worried at first that her longsword would also pose a danger to her allies in the confines of the corridor, but Axel turned and ran to open the door. As the first soldier reached her, Amiel caught his strike on her small shield. She swore as she heard it crack down the middle, threw the now-worthless shield aside and attacked. The soldier's heavy armour restricted his movements. She had studied this armour as the men followed, and while good for heavy protection, no armour was flawless. With a cry, she slammed a two-handed blow to the knee joint of her enemy's armour, feeling its weaker join give way and her blade hack into flesh. The man fell without a cry. He remained silent even as she thrust her blade through his throat.

Beside her, Jenvilno slid around an attack and stepped in close. His masked face almost touching the helm of his enemy, he grabbed the man's sword arm and wrenched him off-balance. His pale eyes blazed as he slammed his short-sword under the soldier's arm and into his chest. Tearing his blade free, he released his grip on the guard's arm and let him fall. He slowly stepped over the corpse as he took on his next adversary. The blade flashed again, and Amiel gasped as an otherworldly light seemed to bleed from the sword in pulses. She remembered how it had glowed, even in the dark forest.

"*Lux.*" She had time to breathe before another man struck at her, and she rejoined the fight. She killed him quickly, but another took his place, and she knew that she and Jenvilno couldn't last long like this. Next to her, the masked man smashed his opponent's sword away and buried his own blade in the unprotected throat. As the man fell, soundless, he dropped his own sword and clutched the blade in his throat. He dragged it from Jenvilno's grip, and before the masked man could retrieve it, he was lost under the trampling feet of the next soldier.

"Take another sword!" Amiel ordered. Instantly she regretted the panic which made her give commands to the saint beside her. Jenvilno shook his head slowly, his eyes never leaving the mass of enemies.

"Step... forward... and... try..." his voice ground from his throat as he faced them down.

His fists came up before his face, the left poised higher to strike. His eyes shone with their wild light. Amiel began to panic again. Was he insane? Did he hope to defeat them all with his bare hands? A cry was dragged from her when Jenvilno darted forward and to one side, around a flashing sword. His left fist drew back, and hammered forward an instant later. The soldier before him somehow made no noise as Jenvilno's knuckles crushed his jaw. The force of the blow slammed the man to one side. His head struck the wall, his helm ringing against the stone. His neck twisted to a grotesque angle with a crack, and he lay unmoving. Amiel engaged another soldier, forced him back into his fellows with all her strength, and together they fell back a little. Jenvilno followed them, pressing forward like a mad dog. He sidestepped around more attacks; left, then right. His fist shot out again, smashed a man's lips into crimson tatters. He dodged around another blade, and struck again, this time with his right fist. His strength was almost abnormal, frightening. He struck again, and again; brutal and precise. Each time his fists caused terrible damage. But the soldiers before him were too many and, even if armed, he and Amiel could not win.

A merciful blast of cold air told Amiel that Axel had finally forced the bar and opened the door. She backed away swiftly, sacrificing the cramped quarters, knowing they needed the escape route. In front of her, Jenvilno twisted and shifted his feet. His right fist caught another exposed jaw in a ferocious, hooking punch. His latest victim staggered back against the others, and Jenvilno too backed away. He crouched long enough to retrieve his sword from the dead man's flesh, and then he was beside Amiel again, retreating with her. Amiel stole a glance over her shoulder, and saw that Jotun's word had been good for one thing, at least. Behind her, the promised boat waited, floating in the shallows of the wide river. It was held by only one rope, which Axel sawed at with a knife.

Amiel turned back to the gateway. Soldiers spilled out of it, more and more of them. But something was different. Their weapons were sheathed now and their terrible, silent attack was just a memory. She saw Jenvilno now, one soldier held by the throat, apart from all the others. The man must have fought him and been defeated. He now offered no resistance as the masked man found a gap in his armour and gutted him. Jenvilno dropped the dead man and moved toward the boat. The soldiers moved forward as one again, but they made no move to strike. Without a word, they began to form back into their rigid column. Amiel too moved to the boat and took her place in it beside Axel. Jenvilno stepped in as Axel finally cut away the last strands of the rope. The current took the boat and they began to float away. Amiel looked down to return her sword to its scabbard.

"What was that?" Axel asked. Amiel looked into his strained eyes, saw the fear of a civilian untested in true combat. "Why did they just attack like that? Why didn't they say anything? Why didn't they scream?"

"I don't know." Amiel knew not to show it, but she was disturbed by it as well. No battle cries, no shouts, no screams of pain or fear as she and the masked warrior tore among them with blade and fists. What sort of men were they?

A set of oars lay on the floor of the boat. With a glance at Amiel, Axel took the rower's bench and picked them up. He began to row, his slender arms straining each time they entered the water.

A soft movement made them both look, in panic, toward the other end of the boat. But it was only Jenvilno. His eyes swept over them, not seeing them, as he turned his back and stood motionless at the prow. His lean figure stood black against the mist ahead.

At first there was only the soft sound of the oars entering and leaving the water, but Amiel started when she heard a hissed curse from Axel. His rowing lost its rhythm.

"Axel, what-" she began to ask.

"*Look,*" he said. "*Look* at them."

The riverside was lined with silent soldiers. The two with halberds stood at the centre, and along the entire length of the bank their army waited, watching the three in the boat. They stood in the same way; left hand on the hilt of their swords, right fisted and held to their chests. Light from the morning sun struggled through clouds above, glinting from their armour. The line of soldiers stretched from the wall beside the gatehouse, along the river to the thick line of trees the boat now approached. The carcass of some great animal lay in the water. Crows screamed as they fought and picked at the dead flesh, but other than that there was no sound, the soldiers only watched.

The boat passed into the trees.

Chapter Nine

"We hardly 'parted as friends' there, wouldn't you say?"

Amiel had a retort ready for Axel's glib remark, but she bit it back when she saw how frightened the boy was. He paused in his rowing and tried to grin at her, but the silent soldiers had marked him as they had her, and the smile dropped from his lips.

"He left us the boat," she said softly. "They must have been acting against his orders."

"You think so?" said Axel, "you don't think maybe his fear of Decius got the better of him and he changed his mind?"

"You heard him. He was a good man, he was tired of Decius. He let us through."

"Then where was he? Where did he go?"

"I don't know. But we are through, and there was no fight. Not with him, anyway."

"You still think we are in your story, don't you?"

The question was asked earnestly, and Amiel felt no anger this time. She met Axel's eyes.

"How else do you explain it? A giant who let us through without a challenge. The names, the sword."

"Oh yes. Janvier owned a sword too. It must be him. What about the sword?" Axel said.

"Janvier's great-sword, *Lux*. Did you not see it glow as he struck the soldiers down?"

"I saw a blade that flashed in the morning sun. Nothing more. And that is hardly a great-sword. It's more like the ones your infantry carries. Do you have anything else, or just coincidences and vague similarities?"

"He told us Decius was the Mad King. He also told us the Great Trickster awaits us next, exactly as in the story. They are more than just similarities."

"So, he has heard your story too. He also told us he would see us off. He told us we could have safe passage."

"Perhaps all of the details are not quite correct," Amiel admitted. "But it is still him." She glanced at the saint, lowered her voice. "He is still Janvier. Did you see him fight?"

"Yes," Axel said, and his voice dropped too. "Is it like a saint to fight so brutally?"

"He is a knight," Amiel told him. "He must fight and kill, though he doesn't enjoy it."

"A strange assessment of someone who loses his sword, then fights on with his fists rather than retreating," Axel said.

"You were still unlocking the door. Nothing I can say will convince you. You will see as we get closer to Deseme."

"*Decius*. His name is Decius," Axel fell silent for long moments after this. His voice was still hushed when he spoke again. "I almost fainted when Jenvilno talked."

A weak attempt at humour, but welcome following the disturbing fight with the soldiers. Amiel dutifully smiled.

"I still can't pin down his voice, his accent."

"I know what you mean," the youth said. "He speaks like a nobleman, but it's different at the same time. It's almost like in the old plays from a hundred years ago, or more."

Amiel paused, thinking. Axel was right. There was something archaic in Jenvilno's voice, his speech patterns. His voice sounded like wind through ruins, and his words seemed torn from the pages of some ancient history. How old was he? She remembered his explosive speed and furious strength, and she knew the saint inhabited a young body. But of course, he still spoke in the manner of his time, from centuries ago. Again, she gripped the glass shard, as the boat ploughed on through the water.

"And there was that fighting style too," Axel's voice again cut through her thoughts. "I heard about fist-fighters like that. The guard, the perfect footwork. It's like the old arena-fights they used to have in the Holy City."

Amiel nodded agreement, annoyed she had missed that. She had spent time at the Holy City of *Theos*, the capital of the Empire. She had done some of her training there, and served as a soldier on its colossal walls and fortifications. In her spare time, she had studied the history of the city. The great arenas, used now for chariot races and plays, had in less refined times been stages for lethal fist fights and weapon combat. She had only briefly touched upon the histories of the fist fights, but she knew it was a graceful yet devastating art. Jenvilno's guard-stance came to her again, the fast movements, the crushing blows. Speed and economy, precision and power. Here was a man with strict training. But the fighting art had flourished in the centre of the Empire, and Janvier had lived around here, far to the west. How had he learned to fist-fight in that way? Amiel didn't know. Perhaps the saint had travelled in his ancient days. Stories about him were numerous, but far from definitive. She stole another look at the masked man. His eyes were unfocused, staring at nothing. How could Axel doubt this was the saint? Amiel still felt a chill being this close to him; almost touching the otherworldly, the divine. Even before she had known he was beyond human, she had felt it. Now she knew he was Saint Janvier, it all made sense. She knew Axel would believe too, once they reached the next gate.

Chapter Ten

Axel was enthusiastic in his rowing, but he was a civilian and his lack of physical conditioning began to show before long. Without comment, Amiel held out a hand as she saw his strength flagging, his breathing laboured. Raising no objection, he stood and handed her the oars so she could take his place. Before she turned to sit down, she glanced ahead to where the river was taking them.

Far away, where the river thinned to a silver wire and the trees either side were a confusion of deep green, black shapes began to struggle from the fog.

Amiel's mouth lifted in a smile as the great hulks shrugged off their shrouds of mist and stood proud, marking the edge of her world. The great black mountains, each one reaching for the sky itself, formed another wall across the river. They ran from north to south, cutting off the rest of the continent from the civilisation further east. No one knew what lay beyond them. The uncharted forest they struggled through now was hostile enough. Still, explorers had tried to break through the trees and climb over the mountainous barrier awaiting them. Some had even returned, with tales of impassable slopes and furious storms driving them back. They must have been lying, she realised. As first they would have had to pass through Jotun's gate, which not one of them had mentioned. Attempts to sail around the mountains had been met with inhospitable rock shores and impossible landings. Sailing was a risky venture at all times, the ships needing to cling to the coast and the captains reluctant to risk the open water. The harsh shores beyond the mountain belt meant that the lands to the west were still unexplored.

The titans before her had a rich presence in local

stories. Visible from her town on rare clear days, black against the light sky, they were known as the Towers. Pre-*Theos* pagans had believed them to be the home of their gods, their deadly terrain and harsh weather meant to keep uninvited humans away from the divine. They believed each one was home to a different god, and named each peak after the god's domain. These names remained, though the names of the deities themselves had been lost after the Conquest of *Theos*.

Amiel looked at each visible peak in turn, from left to right, trying to remember their names. Love, Death, Sun, Stars, Ocean, Thunder, Forest, War, Harvest... she didn't know which name belonged to which mountain. Except for the one ahead of her, the one the river was leading them directly to. Greatest of all the mountains, at the centre of the line; its mighty black peak broken in two by some ancient cataclysm, giving the appearance of horns, that one was Law. Why had the ancients chosen Law for the biggest and mightiest of the mountains? Perhaps their god of law had been king over all the others, and had taken the most majestic tower at the centre for his own. Other names for the mountain could be found in other western towns and villages, but all pointed to the same realm: Justice, Trial, Judgement. The ancients in this part of the Empire were believed to have been simple farmers and hunters, but then Amiel reasoned Harvest or Forest would have taken the central mountain, not one of the lesser spires on either side. A society with Law as its backbone must have been more sophisticated than scholars further east in the Empire believed.

She sat and began to row, quickly falling into a steady rhythm. As the oars entered and left the water, she wondered now about the names of the forgotten gods. She wondered what forms they had taken, how they had loved and fought together in their myths. They were gone now. Lost under the jealous rule of *Theos* –

His name itself only a word for "God" in a long-dead language. There was no pantheon for *Theos*. No wives, brothers or children to venerate or defy Him. There was no God but Him. He existed alone, at once everywhere and, to her mind, distant from humanity far below him. She recalled a handful of stories where He appeared, speaking as a disembodied voice, from the throats of animals or in the roar of thunder or raging water. These dead gods each took a mountain as their home, *Theos* took the entire universe.

Amiel glanced around at Jenvilno, unmoving like a grim figurehead at the prow. The black mountains loomed before him, the old gods looking down on the saint. Not cowed by the god-mountains, he stood alone against them. Where did the saint's mind wander? What was he thinking of? The end of the river, of course, the Mad King awaiting them, their quest concluded. She looked up again at the Towers. She didn't know how they were going to bypass the great mountains, but she knew they would succeed where so many others had given up or died. The days of the old gods were long over, and they would not stop the saint.

Chapter Eleven

After hours of rowing, the mountains seeming no closer, night began to fall.

Amiel needed to rest, but she did not want to seem impudent by telling the saint when to stop. Did Jenvilno even need to rest? Did his body tire as normal ones did? She had heard stories of flowers blooming where Janvier walked, and his entire body glowing with a soft light. But obviously this was not the case with this Jenvilno incarnation. From what she had seen, though incredibly strong and dangerous, the masked warrior was fully human, and subject to all the rules that implied.

Her disquiet vanished when Jenvilno himself turned his grey gaze upon her, no longer facing ahead. His meaning was clear and she angled the boat to a likely landing spot on the shore. As the boat touched down, Amiel dropped the oars, leapt out and grabbed the rope. She hastily lashed it to a tree stump near the bank, and the boat halted as it ran fully aground. Axel and Jenvilno joined her on land, and together they fought into the trees, looking for a camping spot. They found one in a small clearing not far into the woods, crossed by a small stream that trickled down to feed the river. Amiel quickly gathered enough wood for a fire, while Jenvilno sat on a rock, silent. As Amiel struggled to light the fire, Axel crept off to the edge of the trees.

"Where are you going?" Amiel asked.

"I thought I would catch us some food," the boy answered. "It's been a long time since the feast with Lord Ogre."

Amiel ignored his joke. The fire caught; she stood up and faced him. "Be careful. We don't know if Decius or the Trickster have men in the forest around here. Or what animals you might find. Do you think you can catch something without getting yourself killed?"

"I suppose that depends," Axel said. "Is there anything in your story about a handsome young rogue dying on a hunting trip?"

She was on the verge of an irritated retort when Axel held up a conciliatory hand.

"A joke, nothing more." He dug through the pockets of his coat, eventually producing a length of wire. "I hunt like a coward, so I should be safe. I'll set some snares and then you can enjoy my company until we catch something. A bit of luck, and we should eat well."

Axel crept into the trees, and Amiel took a seat on a fallen log opposite Jenvilno. The firelight flickered on the metal of his mask, and threw the eye holes deep into shadow. He had removed his sword-belt, and the short blade rested against the rock he sat upon. The saint sat truly motionless, his hands hung between his knees. After a few moments, Axel returned to sit beside Amiel. Tired from the day of travelling, none of the three spoke until suddenly Axel stirred beside Amiel.

"Something in one of the traps," he said with a smile. Amiel had heard nothing, even with her keen soldier's ears, but she was glad when Axel stood and vanished into the forest again. She had stupidly not eaten at Jotun's feast, so distracted had she been. She hadn't eaten since before entering the forest, and her stomach was painful with hunger. Amiel knew she couldn't be so careless again. It was impossible to know how long the trip to the Mad King would take, and it was important to eat whenever the opportunity presented itself.

Axel returned, the body of a fawn in one hand. The bloody wire was in the other, and he slid that back into his pocket as he re-joined the other two at the fire. Amiel took the carcass from him and gutted it swiftly. She cooked it over the fire and, when it was ready, began to divide it into three parts. She and Axel took theirs, and while the youth began to tear into his, Amiel held the third portion toward Jenvilno. The masked warrior's head lifted enough for him to look at her, the shadows falling away to reveal his eyes. He stared through her for a few heartbeats, then once again his head lowered. Amiel placed the leftover meat on the log between Axel and herself, knowing they could finish it between them. The boy had not noticed the strange moment passing between her and Jenvilno. She remembered now that Jenvilno too had not eaten at the feast, and now he ignored the food before him. She found herself again questioning the rules the saint had to live by in his human form. Could he survive without eating? Had he crept back to the feast and eaten his fill? She dismissed both of these possibilities. She could hear him breathing behind the mask, it followed that he needed to eat as well. And she did not believe he would remove the mask to eat. She thought about the myth of his final quest, the vow he had made not to remove his helm. With the mask serving as his helm, preventing him from eating, Amiel reasoned Jenvilno must have made a holy vow to *Theos* as well, to fast until the quest was done. At first, she worried about his strength failing, but she chided herself for this lack of faith. *Theos* would not allow his soldier to fail, provided his belief remained strong. Still, the journey to the stronghold of the Mad King could not be a long one, a few days or a week at most, she guessed.

She tore into the meat in her hands, trying to slow her eating and largely failing. It was unseasoned and conditions were hardly ideal out here in the wilderness, but she was hungry enough to enjoy it. She smiled to herself, it was no worse than her cooking at the very heart of civilisation. Amiel didn't know what she would have been if not a soldier, but it would not have been a chef.

"What awaits us next?" Axel asked, cutting through

her thoughts. "Tell me about this Trickster Jotun mentioned."

"You knew so much about the first gate, why do you need to ask?"

"The rumours I heard only mentioned the first gate. What lies beyond is a mystery to everyone. Must be that no one managed to pass beyond Jotun. What does your story say?"

Amiel scanned his face for signs of mockery, but Axel seemed sincere. She thought back to when she had last heard the story. As she began to speak, she stole a glance at Jenvilno across the flames. He wasn't listening.

"The second of Deseme's generals is known as the Great Trickster," she said. "He isn't fast or strong, but he is clever. He will try to trick Janvier, but it won't work. Janvier will outwit the Great Trickster himself."

Axel glanced over to where Jenvilno sat, apart from them both. When he turned back to Amiel, one eyebrow was raised.

"Outwitted in four words or less," he said. "I almost wish it were true."

Amiel sighed and shook her head. He had made such a valiant effort not to be obnoxious. The night was clear, so there was no need for a shelter. She lay on the ground beside the fire, wrapped in her cloak, and closed her eyes. She heard Axel lie down as well, but no sound from Jenvilno.

Chapter Twelve

Another day of travelling brought them to the base of the great mountain, Law.

It grew taller and taller as they approached, the cracks and gashes in its black edifice becoming visible as they drew close enough to see through the mist. Vegetation and scrub clung to the lower slopes, but as it plunged upward through the fog and clouds, its stones grew bare. This close to the colossus, Amiel could no longer see the top when she glanced over her shoulder. How were they going to traverse such a great barricade in their path?

As they sailed closer still, Axel gently touched her arm. He pointed, and she had her answer. "Look," he said. "There's an opening in the face of the mountain. The river flows right into it."

Amiel followed his hand. His eyes must have been sharp, because it was almost half a minute before she could see what he saw. He was right. At the base of the mountain, the river flowed into a crack in the rock, vanishing into blackness. It had been invisible against the side of the mountain, but now she saw it as an even darker patch against the stone face. The opening was pointed at the top, shaped almost like one of the lancet windows on the Church of Janvier.

"Those are the God Mountains, aren't they?" Axel asked. "The Towers? Do you think that tunnel leads all the way through?"

Amiel strained her eyes. She thought she could almost see into the entrance. The current carried them forward in its sluggish flow, though she paused in rowing. As they covered the final few metres, Amiel saw jutting rocks in the water around the opening. The danger was great for their small boat, but her rowing was skilful; honed by silent night infiltrations across fortress moats and along hidden underground waterways in occupied cities. She guided them expertly through the cracks and past the rocks.

They were in the mountain, within Law. Amiel could hardly believe it. She expected to feel crushed, aware of the vast weight of rock and earth over them. But instead she felt at peace in the darkness. She felt safe. She inhaled, drew the breath of the mountain deep into her lungs. The current carried them enough now, and she placed down the oars and stood with Axel. The air was cool, and she tasted minerals floating on it. Adrift in the blackness, she felt the presence of Axel beside her, but she saw and heard nothing other than the soft noise of the water. For some minutes they continued like this, deeper into the roots of the mountain, and it was with regret Amiel noticed the darkness beginning to lift.

Light from torches, set along the walls of the rock tunnel, fought back the shadows. In the light of their flames, Amiel looked around her in new amazement. The tunnel's walls were smooth, worn down by uncountable years of running water. Tiny grains of crystal sparkled in the torch flames, stars buried in stone, and opposite her, Jenvilno's mask reflected the blackness, broken by a thousand points of light.

Along the walls, scraped into the stone, Amiel saw many lines and shapes, forming half-familiar patterns. They clustered together, the symbols forming horizontal lines, arches, grids and spirals. She realised they were ancient letters. Runes, she thought they were called. It was a long time since she had studied the language of runes, and she caught only glimpses of them, impossible to read. She could only stare at them, cut into the walls, the darker lines of the letters sparkling with embedded crystal.

"Beautiful," Axel murmured beside her.

She smiled. "Yes," she told him.

"Yes, what?" his smile was a little uncertain.

"It goes through. The tunnel goes through the mountain."

"How do you know?"

"Why else would there be torches? We're here," she told him. "We've reached the second gate. It's in this mountain."

Axel was about to say something, probably to disagree or make some idiotic remark, when a tunnel to their right opened out to a landing area. Cut into the rock, a long, flat bank rose just above the surface. Ahead of them, an iron portcullis barred their way, cutting off further passage into the mountain. Amiel saw all this in a heartbeat, then returned her gaze to the stone bank to their right. It was lined with soldiers.

Their armour was crimson, turned to dim fire by the torchlight playing across the metal. Like Jotun's men, they too wore helmets that hid their faces; cheek and nose guards covering all but their eyes and a sliver of mouth. Amiel's hand rested on the hilt of her sword, but the soldiers on the stone bank did not stare at them, did not seem to be lying in wait. Their weapons were all sheathed, and most of them ran back and forth on the bank, preparing the landing point for the boat. They shouted at one another, and as the boat touched the stone, ropes were thrown to the three travellers to help secure it. Amiel left Axel to do that, his nimble hands swiftly knotting the rope and securing their craft. She watched the soldiers as they worked. They were disciplined, agile and efficient despite their armour, which was again heavier than she was used to seeing simple foot-soldiers wearing. A little behind the others, watching the landing from his own pocket of calm, stood a man with the plumed helmet of an officer. His arms were folded across his slender chest, and even without the black plume on his helm, he stood taller than the men and women securing the boat.

As Amiel stepped ashore, he approached them. His helm was like the others, hinged nose and cheek guards hiding most of his face. Amiel could see his brown eyes, and a neat, dark moustache above his mouth. Little else was visible, but still she found herself relaxing. He did not smile, but his voice was warm when he spoke.

"Welcome, challengers."

Behind him, Amiel could see a passage leading deeper into the rock. The boat fully secured, his men began to form up into a rigid line behind him, stretching down the stone bank.

"We will untie your boat and raise the gate for you," the leader told the three travellers. He looked into Amiel's eyes as he spoke next, "but you know what you must do first."

Amiel nodded. Another gate. It was happening.

"Come now," the man ordered. He led them to the passage, and the stone steps that awaited them at the end of it.

Chapter Thirteen

As Amiel's legs grew tired, the staircase ceased its upward climb, and they found themselves in another long corridor, this one wider. Torches lined the wall on their left, lighting their way. On the other side, a great many weapons were exhibited. Swords beyond count glinted in the torchlight, other less common weapons scattered throughout them. Amiel saw a great, black axe and resisted the urge to touch it. It was majestic, its beauty brutal. Black, decorated with silver runes, and with blades that flared outward, it dominated the centre of the weapon display. Around it, knives, maces, and some lances and spears hung amongst the swords. The weapons ranged from the ostentatious high quality of a nobleman's blade, through the plain but functional weapons of true killers, down to the ugly rust-pitted, nicked blades of peasants.

"The weapons of the previous challengers," the officer told her, without turning around. "Some were good, some were bad. Some had it in them to be truly great. All fell before the Great Lord."

Amiel nodded, though he still did not look at her. Knowing this was the gate of the Trickster, she wondered whether these were truly the weapons of conquered challengers, or if they had merely been put up as an intimidation tactic.

They passed more swords, a few less impressive axes and even a crossbow before they reached the end of the corridor. Another spiral staircase lay there, leading still further into the belly of the mountain.

There were no torches along the wall here, and the officer took one from its bracket on the wall before they again began their ascent. This staircase went on even higher, the spiral wider. Amiel could look over the stone barrier at her side, back down to where they had started their climb. It was quickly lost to shadow as they went higher, and she began to wonder if they were not climbing to the very top of the mountain itself. They couldn't be, she reasoned. They had been climbing for a very long time, but not enough to reach the great split peak of Law. They were still some way below the titanic stone horns.

After almost an hour of climbing, they reached the top of this staircase too. It left them in a small, circular room with walls of smooth stone. Across from them, Amiel saw another doorway. This one was slightly pointed at the top, and once again the officer set off toward it, leading them.

Through the opening, the three travellers found a corridor even larger than the one holding the weapons. The high ceiling was arched, and this time rows of torches lined both walls, though spaced at wider intervals. As the officer led them through the doorway, Amiel saw why this was. There were tapestries hanging on the walls either side, between the torches. They were huge, stretching from the floor to the beginning of the arch's curvature.

Amiel slowed to examine the first one they passed. It showed a slender figure with red hair. He stood on a great mountain, and defied a mighty army below him. A bright sword was in his hand, and the figure's woven face was split in a wide smile. Amiel looked across the passageway to the tapestry on the other side, and this showed the same red-haired figure. At the centre, he stood over the grotesque carcass of a giant. The pictures around it showed the swift thinking he had used to trap and kill his terrible opponent, digging a great pit and tricking his foe into it. Following the others, Amiel looked now at the next set. It became obvious that every tapestry here was some testament to the strength, cunning or charisma of this red-haired man. The tapestry to her left showed him sitting at a long table attended by knights in full armour, his face the only one visible. This time, he looked out of the tapestry at the viewer, and shared his grin with Amiel. His eyes shone green in this tapestry too, brighter than anything around him. Across from this one, the red-haired figure was shown cradling a child amidst a crowd of onlookers, golden light shining around both him and the baby in his arms.

"Who is that?" Axel asked, reaching out to touch one of the hangings.

"These show some of the many deeds of our great lord," the officer told him. "Please do not touch them, they are very valuable."

"Of course they are," muttered Axel. "Can you imagine the arrogance of someone who would cover his walls with pictures of himself?"

"Now I've met you, it's not too difficult," Amiel said. She expected a retort, but Axel smiled, before looking startled at his own reaction.

"Very occasionally you can be amusing, it seems," he conceded.

They reached the end of the stone corridor, their way barred by huge wooden double doors. They were fashioned from a fine-looking dark wood, their hinges cast in black iron. Two heavy rings of black metal served as door handles. The officer placed his torch in an empty bracket on the wall. He spoke again, his voice softer than before and his face away from them, but still Amiel heard his words as he threw the doors open before him.

"Lord Gwydion awaits."

Mythmaking: Part Two

Janvier will come next to the gate of the Great Trickster. The Trickster is clever and he is sly, but he is also a coward. He is too afraid to fight mighty Janvier. He will try to trick the great knight with his cunning words, to drive him away from the gate into the deep dark forest or into his traps.

But Janvier is clever too, and Janvier is wise. He will use his wits to trick the Trickster, and walk through the gate unharmed.

Chapter Fourteen

The doorway led into a huge cavern, deep within the mountain's core. It had been cut and shaped into a colossal feast-hall, greater than any Amiel had seen in the castles or forts she had been based at. In the centre, a huge number of people stood talking to one another. The walls were merely the bare stone of the cavern walls, smoothed and sanded until they were perfectly flat. More tapestries hung from the walls, and instead of simple torch holders providing light, thick crimson candles burned in golden brackets set in the walls. Further into the room, the shadows deepened. But Amiel could still see another great set of doors at the far end, opposite their entrance. The ceiling was of smooth stone too, a golden chandelier attached to a chain hung over the feast-hall. Dozens of crimson candles burned in this too, flames flickering on the gold. Throughout the room, pillars of thick stone held up the ceiling, simple cylinders carved with the same runes Amiel had seen on the walls in the river passage.

Spaced along the walls, between the candles, Amiel saw statues in the old style of what was now the northern Empire. Great warriors, savage but regal in their furs and chainmail, their helms winged or crested. They held battle-axes, or two-handed swords, a far cry from the delicate statues of poets, artists and statesmen found in what would become the eastern Empire. But it was from the east the soldiers of *Theos* had come. The northern berserkers had fought the ruthless, close-packed legions of *Theos* and lost. Their statues and art destroyed, their people killed or assimilated. These statues, if they were originals, or even if they were good imitations, were worth huge amounts further east in the Empire.

Before the crowd, a long table lay beneath the chandelier. Its top was covered with golden candlesticks, more flames fighting the darkness in the room. The table was empty, the chairs pushed out haphazardly, deserted.

"Do you think he likes gold?" Axel asked, his tone mild.

Amiel wasn't listening. At the edge of the room, a number of minstrels strummed on their instruments. It was a tune she vaguely recognised, an old traditional one. Slow and majestic; when sung, it told the tale of an ancient king whose sons fought for his crown after he died, and their realm had bled. *The Bitter War*, she thought it was called. The instruments the minstrels played were strange, archaic. Their fingers danced across the strings, the notes melancholic. They were lyres, an eastern instrument, not fitting with the very distinct decorations of the hall.

She looked again at the crowd. Dressed in their finest clothes, the men in silk shirts, the ladies in beautiful dresses, their conversation was a low rumble over the music. Amiel tried to see their faces, but all of them were turned away from her, facing back into the darkness of the deep hall or speaking to one another.

All except one. A tall man stood at the centre of the crowd. He wore a shirt of crimson, and leggings of deep black leather, tucked into red boots. His red hair was swept straight back from his forehead in a style Amiel believed had been fashionable in the courts of the Empire decades ago. His stance was relaxed, casual. His arms loosely folded, the tall man grinned as he stared at her. His face was long, his chin pointed. Above a blade-like nose, his eyes flashed as they met hers.

Green eyes; it was the man from the tapestries. He raised his hands, and with three claps he had the crowd's attention.

"A moment's silence, please!" he bellowed. His voice

boomed from his thin chest, far stronger than Amiel had expected. The people around him fell silent, and the minstrels stopped playing. He strode toward the three travellers. His step was almost silent, and he seemed to glide over the floor to stand across the table from Amiel. As he reached it, he leaned down, palms on the wood. His green eyes glittered at her from beneath thin, red-gold brows. He was older than she had first thought; perhaps forty-five years were behind him. As he fixed her with his sickle-grin, the other ladies and gentlemen of the hall began to crowd around him, lining his side of the table, facing inward with him at the centre. They clamoured for his attention but he brought silence again with a slam of his palms on the wood. Once more, his voice sounded, slithering from his lips this time.

"I have challengers, it would seem," he murmured. He looked around now at the crowd, his mouth twisting as if he tasted something unpleasant. He held his hands out, palms upward, a dismissive gesture toward the three.

"Three more who dare to face the Great Lord Gwydion. How many have come here, over the long years? How many have fallen before me?"

He shrugged now, mock puzzlement on his face. The others around him laughed. Fast as a whip-crack, lean Lord Gwydion had a dagger in his hand. Rearing up, he spun the blade through swift fingers, the metal as bright as his eyes. He slammed it down into the wood of the table, leaning his full weight upon it, his other hand splayed on the surface as he leered at Amiel.

"Too many!" he hissed, though still he smiled, a fierce good cheer in his words. "Challengers beyond count! They came with their strength and their armour and their mighty weapons, and one by one did they fall before me. Their sharp swords, their fabled axes, their hammers and spears and maces, you've seen them all out there on the walls. Not one could match the power of

Great Gwydion, wielding only this simple little dagger!"

"Rammed in their backs while they were sleeping, was it?"

Gwydion's grin faltered a little, his mouth twisting, but when his eyes slid over to Axel, his mouth widened once more. Amiel too looked at the youth beside her. His eyes glowed with their strange, hungry light. Just as they had done when they first met. There was something almost predatory in the slender boy's eyes. She felt herself recoil from him as he stared down the red-haired lord.

Gwydion slowly stood upright once more. One hand rose to stroke his chin, while the other cradled his elbow. He cast his eyes left and right, looking at his followers, and one eyebrow rose to his high forehead. When he finally spoke, his voice was soft.

"My, my," he said, the voice of a circling carnivore. "Who speaks such insults to their gracious host? Did one of the warriors bring his pretty wife with him? Could they find no one to watch their little daughter?"

Axel's lips were already moving in a retort, but the men and ladies of Gwydion's court drowned him out with their laughter. Amiel smiled a little herself, though she tried not to. Before she could resume a serious face, she felt Axel's eyes on her. Colour rose in his cheeks as the laughter continued, but Amiel remembered his insults and jibes at her faith, and found it a little hard to be sympathetic to the boy.

Lord Gwydion seated himself now, and his guests followed his example, surrounding the table and taking the empty places. The lord beckoned to the three, his face pleasant once more, boisterous charm returning to his voice as he spoke.

"But why do you still stand? Let it not be said that Lord Gwydion was not a noble opponent. Let no one say he didn't give a warm welcome! Come, sit."

Amiel took the seat directly opposite the lord.

Jenvilno sat to her right. Axel stepped forward, but found no empty chair awaiting him. Gwydion allowed the moment to extend more than long enough for the youth to feel uncomfortable, before he finally leaned up onto the table, looking down to the far end.

"You," he called to a woman sitting at the opposite corner. "My challengers have taken the seats of honour. Make space for their... little friend, would you?"

The woman kicked her chair back and, stumbling as she scurried around the table, vanished through the doors beyond the minstrels. Amiel wondered briefly where she would go, but her thoughts returned to their host as he smiled at Axel.

"You have my permission to sit," he said. "But hat off at the table, son."

Axel remained calm with an effort that was visible to Amiel, and stalked off down to the far end of the table to take his seat. Gwydion made a gesture, and someone reached past Amiel and Jenvilno to set food before them.

Amiel picked at her food, knowing she should eat but suspicious of the Trickster. She saw Axel drain his goblet, ignoring the huge piece of meat set before him and hold it out for more drink. Next to her, Jenvilno only sat and stared at the lord. For a second only, Gwydion met the masked fighter's eyes, then he dropped his own gaze and looked instead to Amiel.

Light from the golden candlesticks flashed from the fire of his hair, illuminated his face as he smiled across at her.

"Well, my dear," he chuckled. "You passed the gate of the mighty Jotun without a fight, did you? How did you manage that one? Bribe him? Charm him? Threaten him? Or did you just persuade him you don't taste very nice?"

He knew. How did he know? He must have had spies following them in the forest. Or among Jotun's men. Amiel met Gwydion's eye, though his unrelenting stare was beginning to make her skin itch.

"He let us through," she told the slender lord. "He said he was tired of Decius and his evil."

"Tired?" Gwydion's words dripped scorn and disbelief, one hand gripping the edge of the table. "Oh yes, of course poor Jotun is tired. His entire life is a busy cycle of sitting, eating, shitting and sleeping. He must be *exhausted.* So, who would have fought the Great Walrus anyway?"

Here the lord flicked his fingers down the table, toward Axel. "Would your golden-haired little nymph have stepped before the Stomach That Walks, or is his blade no sharper than his wits?"

Once again, the ladies and gentlemen around the table all competed to laugh the loudest. Axel's head remained bowed forward as he sat and took their mockery. This time, Amiel felt no temptation to smile. In palaces, castles and courts across the Empire, she had met a thousand men like Gwydion; dripping with oily charm, marching ahead of an army of sycophants, wielding wit as she wielded her blade. She had no time for them.

"No," she told the lord, interrupting his merriment. "No. Jotun would have fought Jenvilno. As you will."

Gwydion looked now into the pale eyes beyond the mask, and Amiel felt grim satisfaction as the smug look finally dropped from the lord's face. Down at the other end of the table, Axel looked happy again at last. She returned her gaze to Gwydion just as he managed to fix his grin back into place.

"Well, we shall see," Gwydion said.

"We bear you no ill will," Amiel said, though she was feeling more and more of it toward the smarming lord by the second. "But we must get through your gate. The reign of the Mad King must end."

"The Mad King?" this time Gwydion laughed long and loud. "What *has* that bloated old troll been telling you?"

The lord's abrasive wit was grating against Amiel's patience now. Her voice was sharper than she wanted it to be when she responded.

"He told us the truth," she snapped. "Decius is a great king, gone mad and fallen into tyranny. We will kill him."

Gwydion was shaking his head, "For a start, *you* will do nothing to Decius. And he is no king."

"Then what is he?" Amiel asked, "Who is Decius?"

"Calm yourself, my dear," Gwydion smiled. "Sit. Eat. Drink. I will tell you the truth about Decius."

Chapter Fifteen

"Before I start, my dear, would you tell me your name?" Gwydion asked.

"If it'll stop you calling me your 'dear', then of course," Amiel answered. "It's Amiel."

"Amiel." Gwydion rolled the word around his mouth like delicately spiced meat. "Well... Amiel, I first met Decius when I was a wandering warrior, feared for my great intelligence and skill with the blade, famed in songs up and down the land."

Amiel looked down the table. Axel caught her eye and gave her his lopsided smile, shaking his head. Amiel chuckled. He believed Gwydion about as much as she did, then. She turned back as a sudden sound cut across the hush of the crowd. Gwydion had kicked his chair back and risen to his feet, one hand clutching the lapel of his shirt, the other gesturing as he spoke.

"I left another city. Its name? I don't remember. I have left so many the same way. Behind me, beaten enemies, broken promises, shattered hearts. Ahead of me, who could say? Not even I. The Great Lord Gwydion walks where he will."

The crowd laughed obediently. Amiel had felt the lord's eyes upon her as he talked about shattered hearts, and she was finding herself increasingly in no mood for merriment. Gwydion moved on with his tale, his gaze raking his audience.

"And so, I strode on, my brilliant mind already considering what awaited me. Did a new war need my stunning mastery of tactics and deception? Did a great tournament of swordsmanship await a man with a fast hand and faster wits? Were there noble ladies yet unloved, awaiting Great Gwydion?" the lord winked at his audience. "Alas, I fear *that* need is never truly fulfilled."

His smile was fierce now, aggressive, as his courtiers laughed around him. He stared, unblinking, at Amiel. His voice dropped lower as he spoke on, almost a growl.

"I came at last to a narrow bridge, spanning a mighty river. It was there that I first met Decius. From either side of the bridge we came, and in the centre we met."

Gwydion drew his dagger once more, idly toyed with it. He cleaned one nail with it, the silence from his audience total. He twirled the blade again, sheathed it with a flourish.

"But there we stayed; the bridge was too narrow for us to pass one another! I asked... *demanded* he step aside and let me through. He would not. And did I, the Great Lord Gwydion consider for even a second letting *him* pass *me*? Of course not! So, there we stood, and there we stayed. For nine hours we railed and raged at one another, as the river too raged below. We argued our cases, we boasted of our exploits. Each of us told the other man why *he* should be the one to step aside. I know what you are thinking. How did Great Gwydion fit his many deeds into just nine hours? It would be impossible of course. Many were the stories left to tell. But after nine hours wasted, one of us came up with a brilliant plan. Of course, it was I, Gwydion, who thought of a way to end our war of attrition. It was I, Gwydion, who had the wits and cunning. And it was wits and cunning I needed, for what I proposed was a contest of riddles."

"Riddles?" Against her will, Amiel found herself drawn into the story. Gwydion's grin widened and he slammed a palm on the wood of the table once more.

"*Yes!*" he bellowed. "The rules were simple. Each of us would ask the other a riddle, and we would alternate until one of us could not answer. I struggled to keep my face unreadable, though my eyes blazed in triumph. Did he not know who stood before him? Had he not heard of how many had tried to match Great Gwydion's guile, and failed? My victory was certain in my mind, and as we began, already I could taste it. For another nine hours we stood, spitting riddles from our lips. Nine more hours we riddled, until at last one of us was unable to answer."

Here Gwydion lifted his hands, a rueful smile on his face, eyes closed against the memory.

"Yes. Unbelievably, it was I. The wits of Sly Decius proved too nimble, even for Great Gwydion. Conceding defeat with grace, I stood to one side to let the victor pass. But Decius only stood, and smiled. He told me he had need of men such as I, clever men of quick and cunning thought. He told me to follow him, and I knew then where the path of the Great Lord Gwydion lay."

Gwydion smoothed down his hair, though it remained flawlessly slicked back. He spoke only to Amiel now, the faces of those beside him faded in the dim light.

"Decius took me to his fort, deep within the forest beyond this mountain, hidden from the eyes of lesser men. Ever since that day, I have served Decius. The Outlaw Duke, Lord of the Thieves. Together, we plot and scheme. Together, we bring his plans to life."

"What are his plans?" Amiel asked.

"To tear down the world itself," Gwydion smiled. "In his mind, it is rotten and corrupt; every realm ruled by cruel, selfish men, driven only by thoughts of wealth and gain. I listened as he said this, and I asked the Bandit Duke why it was any of his concern. I asked him why do you care if these rulers are corrupt and only filling their purses?"

Gwydion leaned forward suddenly, much further than Amiel would have believed possible without twisting his body out of shape. She recoiled before she could stop herself, away from the protruding nose and chin.

"And after a silent moment, Decius answered," snarled Gwydion. "'Why them, and not me?'"

He hurled himself back into his chair. His head rearing back, Gwydion howled his laughter at the ceiling. His guests joined him, and together their laughter made the chandelier tremble. Again and again his hand slammed to the table. At last the crowd quieted once more, and Amiel felt the emerald gaze of the lord crawl onto her flesh again.

"Why them, and not me?" he repeated, chuckling. He leaned his chin on one hand as he looked at her, eyes wide. "And do you know? I had no answer for him. I still don't, for there is no reason. So, we planned together, and we recruited men. Low men. Serpents. Men who will slit their own mother's throat for a copper coin, then kill the person who paid them to see if they have any more. Our army swells by the hour, more and more flocking to his great banner. The jackals, the vultures, the wolves. An army of thieves, waiting only for the moment when they will march forth to take what isn't rightfully theirs."

Gwydion laughed again, but softly this time, venomous. "And then he sent me here. Far away from the army. Far away from him. He said he needed me to wait here, to watch this gate and keep all but the mightiest challengers away. But in secret, he told me the truth. He had long suspected that Jotun's tortured, barely-beating heart was no longer in his duties, and so he needed a trusted man to watch Baron Banquet and... deal with him if necessary. I knew though, he had another reason. He tried to hide it from me, and he did well. But as they say, you can't cheat a cheater, and I am the greatest there ever was."

"What was this other reason?" Amiel couldn't take her eyes from the lord as he danced around words of lies and deceit.

"Come along, now. You know," Gwydion said.

"You were plotting against him?" She asked.

"Clever, clever girl." Gwydion spoke so quietly she had to strain to hear him. Around them, the crowd did the same. "From the very second I was defeated. From the very moment no riddle came to my lips. From that day I have done nothing but make plans, thought of nothing but treachery. I have lied and deceived and tricked, my schemes so subtle I feared I might one day double cross myself."

"Why?" Amiel said.

"Why?" Gwydion echoed her. "It has already been said by Decius himself. He saw the corrupt and the rich, and he asked 'why them, and not me?' But as I listened, I in turn saw *him* and asked myself the same question. Why him, and not me? And again, I could find no answer. He thought I would be loyal? It is not in my nature. Only profit and gain drive Great Gwydion. Plunder and *power!* Now it's his time, but soon dawns the day when he will feel the kiss of my blade. With his army behind me, with their blades cutting my path, soon the name on every tongue will be the Great Lord Gwyd-"

"Enough!"

Chapter Sixteen

The voice rang across the Hall of Gwydion, silencing even the red-haired lord himself. Amiel and Gwydion looked to the source of the noise, as did the other guests. To Amiel's exasperation, she saw it was Axel who had shouted. Before Gwydion could concoct a reply, the golden-haired youth drained his drink and surged to his feet, launching his chair over backward to clatter onto the floor. He climbed up onto the table. Was he swaying slightly? He flipped his hat up and back onto his head with a grin. His eyes were alive with a spark Amiel couldn't look away from, his mouth wide with that uneven smile. Axel began to walk down the long table. He picked his way carefully among the plates and goblets of the other guests, and the still-burning candles in their golden sticks. As he swaggered along, with all eyes upon him, he began to speak.

"For the whole night now I've sat, forced to listen to the ludicrous rhetoric of this bragging bag of bluster." Here Axel gestured toward Gwydion, not deigning to look at him. His eyes scanned the others at the table, looking each of them in turn in the face, as he continued.

"Maybe it's my fault," Axel said with mock sincerity. "Maybe I am too cynical, maybe it is wrong to doubt my gracious host. But does nobody else find it strange that a self-proclaimed great warrior would piss himself in fear at the very sight of a true fighter?"

A murmuring rustled through the guests around the table, rising in volume. Axel held up a hand for silence and, incredibly, they obeyed.

"The Great Lord Gwydion's shrewd eyes have peered everywhere this fine evening," Axel told them. "Up and down the table, at each of his guests in turn, at the fine food before us and most of all, at his own reflection in his vast hoard of tasteless gold. But only once did he glance at the warrior across from him, and quickly he looked away."

Axel grinned at Amiel, gave her a wink. She tried to catch his eye and stop this madness, but he was moving again, walking down the table once more, and his eyes were not upon her.

"You see Decius and you ask 'why him, and not me?' Well, I have an answer for you, Great Gwydion. Because you are a coward! Because you are a liar! Because most of your swordsmanship is done with a comb! I stepped into this damp, misty purgatory to do a little redistribution of wealth. From the treasure room of Decius into my pockets. Now you tell me he is nothing but a penniless outlaw leader, and I have wasted my time?"

Axel grabbed a drink from a startled guest and drained it in one swallow. He wiped his mouth on the sleeve of his coat.

"Don't let me stop you, Gwydion. Really," Axel said. "You just sit there telling your little stories and smoothing your hair down with one fingernail. It looks like everyone else here has an endless appetite for your lies and posturing... but I am *done!*"

With his final word, Axel kicked another golden chalice, sending it flying away deeper into the room. It struck a pillar and clattered to the floor, deafening in the hush around the table. He turned once more and, eyes on the red-haired lord, began to move again.

"Why do you fear our masked friend so much? It must be something truly terrifying. Do you think he will rumple your shirt? Knock your hooked nose off-centre? Beat the smirk from your face?"

Amiel turned to look at Jenvilno for the first time since Axel had interrupted the meal. The masked fighter looked on, impassive. He did not move or take his gaze from the youth on the table. Amiel's eyes jerked back to

Axel as he walked past her place. He reached Gwydion now, crouching slightly to look the red-haired lord in the eye.

"Worry not, Lord of Lies," Axel smiled. "I am rather tempted to relieve you of your fear. We don't need to unleash our masked killer to deal with you."

Gwydion said nothing for a moment. Elbows resting on his table, fingers steepled together, the lord merely looked up at the youth, a smile of his own barely touching his lips. His voice was mild when he spoke.

"Would you care to be specific, as well as annoying?"

"Nothing would make me happier, Gwydion," Axel chuckled. His hand went to the brim of his wide hat, and he tipped his head in mock-salute. "I, Axel Solarius, challenge you for the right of passage."

Gwydion's guests drew in breath. With horror, Amiel turned to the lord to say he didn't speak for them, that Jenvilno was the true challenger. But Gwydion grinned and said, "wonderful, just wonderful." His voice dropped low, but joy dripped from his words. "Ready yourself, then."

"Excuse me?" Axel took a half-step back, hesitant.

"Ready yourself," Gwydion repeated. "We fight here, and now."

And then, the room was in uproar.

Gwydion's followers all clamoured for his attention again, each trying to catch his eye and offer their encouragement. Amiel grabbed at Axel's sleeve. But the boy was spinning gracefully away even as she reached, leaving her unsure if he had deliberately evaded her or not. She shouted his name, but he seemed not to hear. The noise was deafening, until Lord Gwydion again restored quiet.

"*The rules!*" He screamed, and at once his followers fell into a hush.

"The rules," he said, quieter now, "are very simple.

One of you has challenged me. He must fight me. If he wins, whether I live or not, you will be allowed through the gate to continue on your quest through the dark, haunted forest beyond these walls. When I win, and let me assure you he will *not* live, you other two must leave here. Your chance lost, you can never return."

Despair touched Amiel. This was their only chance to pass through the gate? She hadn't seen Axel fight. She had seen him pretend to be injured then stab someone from behind. Looking at his light frame and the way he carried it, she knew he would be unable to best her in a fight, let alone one of Decius' elite generals. If he failed, and her quest was at an end, then Janvier... Deseme... none of it could be true.

She gritted her teeth. It *was* true, she knew it. She would persuade Axel to retract his challenge, and then her Janvier would fight.

"Need time to prepare?" Gwydion asked. "You have oh, I don't know, three minutes."

The noise resumed again as the lord stood. His followers gathered around him, clapping him on the back and shaking him by the hand. Surrounded by this entourage, the red-haired lord walked to the back of the hall and vanished through the far door. The minstrels began to play once more. The tune was regal now, grandiose. One began to sing, the words were about a wandering swordsman named Gwydion, of great skill and agile mind. Axel leapt down from the table, and immediately Amiel was upon him.

"Are you insane?" she demanded. "Are you drunk? What makes you think you can defeat a general of Decius?"

"Well, thanks for your confidence in my abilities, Amiel," Axel laughed. "This 'general' is nothing but a pompous lizard. You'll see. And then you can pick when you apologise to me. This side of the gate or the next."

"You weren't meant to challenge him," Amiel

refused to give up. "It was meant to be Jenvilno. That's how it happens."

"This? Again?" Axel's smile vanished. "Amiel, when will you realise that's just a story?" He turned to the masked warrior. "Jenvilno, will you maybe tell her you're not some knight in shining armour living out a destined daydream?"

"*No!*" Amiel stepped between Axel and Jenvilno, frantic to stop him from hearing Axel's blasphemy. But she faltered when she saw the masked warrior. Jenvilno had pushed his chair back from the table and waited, motionless. Elbows resting on his knees, the fighter's grey eyes stared further into the hall, beyond Amiel or Axel. Both of them slowly turned, and saw.

Gwydion awaited them, and behind him his followers stood in a semicircle. The lord was clad now in crimson armour, a more ornate version of the officer's who had brought them here. The red plates carried intricate northern runes picked out in gold. The light from the candles on the table and the chandelier above glinted from the metal. His face and hair were still uncovered, and his grin was mocking as he watched them. In his hand, he held the knife he had wielded at dinner.

"You're ready? Said your last words? Maybe had a final drink? Good. Let us begin."

Axel nodded, but before he stepped forward, he turned to Amiel.

"When I win," he murmured, "you'll see."

She said nothing, but beyond them Gwydion grew impatient.

"Come, come now!" he called. "Step forward, and face the Prince of Tricksters!"

Chapter Seventeen

As the last word left Gwydion's lips, Amiel tried to reach forward to stop Axel. How could he not see? How did he not believe it was happening around them? But her arm was numb, her fingers cold, and Axel swaggered over to face Gwydion where he stood. A presence next to Amiel made her turn, and she saw Jenvilno stride past her, over to where the fight would take place. She followed him, and stood next to the masked warrior as the half-circle of Gwydion's followers spread out and closed around the two combatants, finally making a full circle. Within the ring of spectators, Axel and Gwydion faced one another. Gwydion grinned at his opponent, green eyes sparkling.

"It's not too late, you know. You can still run away. You can still hide behind the woman and that masked freak."

Axel smiled back. "Nowhere for you to run, though. Maybe that's why you're trying to talk me out of this."

Gwydion's empty hand reached over his shoulder. He drew a short-sword from a scabbard hidden on his back. Two blades in his hands now, his armour like dark flames in the shadowy hall. He began to advance.

"I think I'll cut your tongue out first," he told Axel. His young opponent began to move too, and together they circled in the space the crowd gave them.

"I'm fairly sure you said you defeated all your challengers with only your knife," Axel drew his own dagger as he spoke.

"And around about now, most of them noticed I was lying," Gwydion smirked. "It's obvious you're quite slow, but did you really trust a trickster to keep his word?"

"Insults won't make me lose my head, *lord*," Axel's laugh sounded a little forced to Amiel. "If you want to beat me, you'll have to outfight me."

"Oh, I intend to," Gwydion's voice was calm, the words slow. But the attack he launched as he spoke was ferocious.

He lunged toward Axel, both blades licking out and seeking the youth's flesh. Amiel gasped as the lord moved with a speed she would never have believed possible. She thought back to the lethargic Gwydion, sitting amongst his sycophants, but she couldn't reconcile that image with the crimson-clad warrior who attacked Axel in a flash of metal.

The youth's knife-work was good as well. In fact, it was excellent. Amiel had fought and killed dozens of knife-fighters during her military deployment, and Axel would have been among the more troublesome ones. He kept his knife-hand back, his other one held out to block and guard against attacks. His footwork was remarkable, almost graceful. His movements seemed flowery and a little ostentatious compared to the brutal economy of Jenvilno's sword and fist-fighting, but he moved well and Amiel allowed herself to be a little impressed.

Axel blocked and dodged, trying to step inside the reach of Gwydion's weapons so he could do damage to the lord's unprotected face and neck. But against an opponent with two blades, armed only with a small knife, Axel was outclassed. Gwydion's sword sliced through the sleeve of Axel's jacket, and the sharp intake of breath from Axel signalled that the metal had found flesh. He jerked with the pain, and his hat fell from his head, landing on the floor between the combatants. Gwydion's knife came up for a killing thrust at Axel's heart, but the youth managed to dance away from the lord and they resumed circling.

"First blood," Gwydion mused, inspecting the tip of his sword, not bothering to look at Axel. His eyebrow rose once more. "You're lucky I didn't poison my blades today."

"I'm grateful, really," Axel said, ignoring the blood leaking from his torn sleeve. "Don't think otherwise just because I'm trying to stab you."

"*Trying*. Good choice of words," Gwydion said. "I don't think you were actually expecting the 'bragging bag of bluster' to know how to fight, were you?"

Axel said nothing. Laughter spilled from Gwydion's throat.

"You just didn't think, did you?" His voice was a snarl, but still he smiled. "You saw the liar, the pompous idiot sat safe in his hall and boasting of his exploits, and you didn't think *that* might have been just another lie!"

He attacked again, this time feinting with his dagger and attacking with his sword. Axel spun away from him, but the motion and his injury conspired to disorient him. Amiel could see he had lost sight of his opponent and screamed for him. Axel whirled, to be met by Gwydion's smug smile,

"Think *really* fast," Gwydion ordered. His blades flashed out, and Axel was too slow.

The youth managed to dodge around the first three strikes, and he blocked the fourth cut, the blade of the sword ringing against his forearm with a metallic clang. Amiel had only begun to wonder why it would make such a sound when Gwydion reversed his slash and found an opening. The lord's short sword opened a shallow cut at the side of Axel's neck, but it was his knife that did the real damage. Gwydion rammed the small blade through Axel's jacket and into the body inside. Amiel heard it strike home in flesh, heard Axel scream as the blade sank into him. Gwydion tore his knife clear and Axel collapsed to his knees, and then forward on his face. Gwydion turned, as the stunned silence of the audience turned into cheers. He raised his knife hand, then swept it downward in a long bow.

"Thank you, why thank you," he favoured them all with his smile. "Once again, the Great Lord Gwydion is victorious, and I owe it all to... myself, actually."

Amiel felt the agony of hopelessness. It was over. None of it was true. She turned to look at Jenvilno but he was silent as ever, motionless. He was looking at Gwydion's knife. Amiel now turned her eyes to the blade that had ended Axel's life, and felt despair wash over her anew at the death of the youth she had barely begun to know. She froze, her soldier's eye trying to focus on Gwydion's knife as he laughed and showed off for his crowd.

There wasn't enough blood on it. The tip of the blade was stained crimson, but nowhere near as much as if it had truly been rammed into Axel's body. Gwydion hadn't noticed; he was too busy celebrating. And Amiel said nothing as a shadow crept up behind the gloating lord.

Gwydion must, at the last second, have heard something. He tried to turn, his smile beginning to fade. But this time it was the trickster who was too slow. Axel looped a length of bloody wire from his snares around Gwydion's neck before the lord could face him, and with a brutal twist the golden-haired youth drew it tight. Gwydion screamed and tried to struggle, but Axel's grip on the wire was too strong. He kept it just tight enough to immobilise the lord, without hurting him too much.

"A word of advice no one seems to heed, my *lord*," Axel murmured in his opponent's ear. "*Never* turn your back on me."

"H-how?" Gwydion choked. His eyes wide with fear and agony. "I *killed* you!"

"You killed a piece of meat. Let me be the first to congratulate you."

At Axel's words, Amiel looked over to the floor where the young man had feigned death. There on the floor lay the huge slab of meat Axel had been presented with when he sat down at Gwydion's table. The red-haired lord's blade had torn right through it, and from the pain on Axel's grey face Amiel could see that he had still been injured by Gwydion's attack; just not fatally, as he had pretended.

Gwydion's blades fell to the floor as his hands went to his throat, scrabbling at the wire encircling it. With a grim smile, Axel kicked the back of the lord's legs and forced him to his knees.

"Now, Gwydion. Great Gwydion, famed in song up and down the land. I believe this makes me the victor. And I believe you should have something to say to me and my friends."

"Never! I'll never-" Gwydion's defiance was cut off as Axel tightened the wire. When the young man allowed him some breathing room, Gwydion was truly broken.

"I yield, I yield! You can all go through. Spare me, please! You can take my title too. I'll let you be the Prince of Tricksters!"

"Kind of you, but no thanks." Axel laughed. He suddenly hauled on the ends of the wires, dragging Gwydion over backwards. He turned to the minstrels, still standing at the end of the room. "Strike up a song," he ordered them. "Play one everyone knows."

The musicians said nothing, they hadn't moved from their positions at all. Now they launched into a drinking song Amiel half-remembered, the upbeat notes jarring with the scene in the hall.

"Ah, yes," Axel smiled to himself, "I always did like this one." He looked around, caught sight of his hat on the floor. Reaching down, he twirled it through his fingers before placing it back on his head. He looked again at Gwydion, who had struggled back up to one knee.

"You can keep your title. You can still be the Prince of Tricksters." As Axel spoke, he slipped something from his sleeve into his awaiting hand. Amiel realised what else he had taken from the table, what had made the noise when the blade struck his arm. She realised she might have been badly wrong about the man standing over the lord.

Gwydion struggled to his knees. He looked up to see Axel standing over him, a heavy golden candlestick in his hand.

"Now," Axel's hand clenched around the weapon, "bow to your king."

The first blow smashed into Gwydion's mouth.

Chapter Eighteen

A new boat awaited them the next morning, their old one gone.

Crafted from white wood, it floated low in the dark water. This one was larger, and boasted a small mast hung with a crimson sail. Amiel walked along the stone dock and paused to look at it, impressed. They would certainly be travelling in more comfort on the way to the next gate. She guessed this meant the next gate was further away, and they had longer to travel. No matter. They would reach it when they reached it.

She stepped from the dock into the boat, legs adjusting quickly to the shifting and rolling of the water. She turned and held out a hand. Behind her, Axel took it with a grateful smile. Lacking Amiel's sure-footedness, he stumbled as he stepped into the boat, but Amiel held him up. Still, he hissed with pain, and she looked at him with concern. She wondered if his injuries were troubling him more than he was letting on.

"I'm fine," he said, seeing her worry and waving her away. "But thank you."

She nodded, returned his small smile, and looked toward the back of the boat. She almost collided with Jenvilno. The masked warrior stood motionless, uncomfortably close. She had not heard even a whisper of a footstep as he boarded. She stepped around him, and he walked past, moving to the prow of the bone-white boat. Amiel stared back at him. She could still not quite reconcile in her mind that this was truly her saint, who she had prayed to in difficult times over the years. She had believed he was somewhere beyond, listening, answering, but now she knew him in the flesh. She had not imagined him so cold and aloof. This did fit with the Gospel of Janvier as she thought about it, though.

Janvier was the Saint of Knights, of Soldiers. He helped those with the strength and will to help themselves. He would not lead her by the hand up the river to Decius.

Dragging her mind back to the present, she looked now to the stone bank. Two scarlet-clad soldiers stood to attention there. Before she could say anything, one of them nodded in her direction. He turned, and called a command into the doorway they had taken last night, when they climbed to the core of the mountain.

Some ancient mechanism began to grind and shriek, and before their boat the iron portcullis began to rise inch by inch. The other soldier on the bank crouched down, untying the pale rope that held them still. With their mooring gone, and a stronger current than before beneath them, the boat began to drift forward, further into the tunnel.

At first, total darkness fell as they passed beneath the roots of the mountain. From this blackness, they slid into the endless white of mist as they left the cave. Thicker than before, it slid around them, probed their throats with swirling fingers. Amiel felt a breeze at her back, and moved to unfurl the sail. Axel helped her, and together they opened it, revealing another golden rune on the crimson sail.

"You know, at this point I'm surprised he didn't lend us a boat made of gold," Axel said.

Amiel smiled, surprising herself. "Why are you still here?" she asked, not unkindly. "I expected you to be charging back out of the forest right now with a few sacks of his gold."

"I was going to," Axel told her. "But, and you'll need to ready yourself for a shock here, when I checked his gold after the fight, all of it seemed to be cheap metal painted with a thin gold veneer. Worthless."

Amiel smiled wider, "well, that certainly fits with the man's personality."

Axel moved to the stern and gripped the boat's

tiller, keeping its course straight on the hidden river they travelled. With one final look at Jenvilno, still standing at the prow, Amiel joined Axel where he sat.

"How do you feel?" she asked him.

"Sore," he admitted. "He was an arrogant son of a snake, but he knew how to fight. Then of course, you finished the job with your heavy-handed battlefield surgery."

Amiel looked up sharply, but Axel was grinning at her without malice. Again, she was surprised to feel a smile on her lips.

"I was stitching your wounds, you ingrate."

"Stitching them, were you? I was beginning to think he had paid you in fake gold to give me a slower death than he ever could. I'm no physician, but I don't think the stitch-marks are meant to be bigger than the wounds."

"I was helping you get some scars," Amiel said. "With a few of those you'll have no trouble impressing the young ladies in all these bars you frequent."

"You think so?"

"Oh, yes. Especially the ones who are already drunk. And desperate. And blind."

Axel glowered at her in mostly mock annoyance.

"Next time, I won't let you near me," he told her.

"You think leaving you to bleed will bother me?" she retorted with a smile.

"Stop smiling at me," Axel replied. "It's really frightening. It reminds me of those big fish with all the teeth that circle and circle before they finally bite."

Amiel was about to respond when a voice cut across theirs.

"Travellers!"

It came from behind them, and high up. Amiel and Axel turned and strained their eyes to see through the mist. At first it was difficult, but at last the white wall drifted apart and both of them drew in a breath of surprise at what they saw.

Carved into the side of the mountain, cut deep into the black rock itself, was a great set of battlements. It thrust out from the mountainside, hanging over the river like a balcony. Its edge was crenelated, and a red flag flew from a golden pole at the centre of the semi-circular edifice. Beside the golden flagpole stood a crimson-clad figure. The great structure rose much too high above them for Amiel to see the man's face, but she knew from the voice it was the herald, the officer who had escorted them to the Hall of Gwydion.

He spoke on, his words rolling down the mountainside to them. "Travellers! Wherever you go, let it be known: the Great Lord Gwydion is dead!"

The man spoke no more. Perhaps the mist closed then, or perhaps their distance grew too great to see, but the battlement was once again lost to their sight, buried in the swirling whiteness. Amiel stared hard at the mist, seeking the stronghold she had seen seconds before, but there was nothing. The news was a surprise, but truth to tell she had not liked Gwydion at all, and didn't much care.

"I didn't mean to."

The words were soft beside her, but Amiel still jerked with surprise, one hand going to her sword-hilt. She hadn't considered Axel. The boy sat by the tiller, looking up at her. His face was pale, and his eyes shone with a fragile light.

"I didn't... I didn't mean to."

Amiel stared for a while at him. "You haven't killed anyone before, have you?"

Axel said nothing, shook his head. Amiel sighed. It made sense. The stories he had told her; dancing, drinking, evading watchmen. For a boy of his age, there had been a lack of stories about fighting, a lack she should have noticed.

Theos army training had prepared Amiel well for her

first kill, and the many that had followed. She didn't understand Axel's feelings, and there existed between them a chasm she did not think she could cross. Still, she tried. She thought back to Axel's victory, and the beating he had given Gwydion. Four or five blows to the face and neck, and this from a slender youth with far more speed and brains than power. The candlestick had been heavy, but Gwydion had been a fighting man, and she had seen weaker men take worse. She had administered worse on numerous occasions, and she had intended the recipients to survive. Her calm eyes met his frantic gaze.

"You are right, Axel," she told him. "What you did shouldn't have killed him, but it did. Wounds are strange like that sometimes."

"I didn't want to kill him." Axel's voice was barely a murmur now. Amiel was lost for a second, her mind blank as she searched for a way to reassure him. Then she smiled as the answer struck her. He had to believe now. It fit perfectly.

"You didn't," she rested a hand on his shoulder. "It was his fault."

Axel's face was unreadable as he looked at her. "What do you mean?"

"He goaded you into challenging him," she answered. "If he had fought Jenvilno as he was supposed to, he would have survived. He deviated from the myth, and he died."

Axel surged to his feet, jerking away from her. Her hand fell from his shoulder as anger burned away the remorse in his eyes. "Still this delusion, Amiel? Still this daydream? That's your consolation? When will you abandon this fantasy? We are not in a storybook with a magic knight, though you seem not to have noticed. What also slipped by you apparently is that it wasn't Jenvilno who got us through that gate. It was *me*. And I didn't do it with words and riddles, I did it with *these*."

He thrust his hands toward Amiel, one of them bearing the small defensive wound from Gwydion's knife.

Amiel knocked his hands aside, irritated, so she could look him in the eyes. She glanced at Jenvilno, worried he would overhear them. But the masked fighter gave no sign of listening. He stood at the prow of the boat, his back to them, staring out across the water. Still, she lowered her voice as she rounded on Axel.

"Gwydion called himself the Prince of Tricksters," she said. "And you defeated him with a trick."

"You can't just explain everything away with a vague reference to your story!" Axel snapped, though his voice had dropped too. "I fought, not Jenvilno. Explain that. The first general's men attacked us. Explain that. We've seen two generals, and heard two completely different stories about just who Decius is. Can you explain that as well with a tenuous link to your legend?"

"Can you explain the similarities?" Amiel countered.

"I don't have to," Axel said, calmer now but unmoveable. "They are coincidences. Or at worst these people have heard your little story and are as bizarrely entrenched in it as you. Or better yet, Gwydion was just lying for the fun of it. He *was* a trickster, as you say."

"Explain why they let us through, then," Amiel said.

"Why... what?" Axel faltered.

"If this is just coincidence, or if they have merely heard the story, why go through the formality of the challenge? Why abide by its rules? What do they stand to gain by doing that? Better yet, if their mission is to guard the gates, why let us even get to the challenge? Why not just kill us? Why go through any of it at all, unless it is real?"

"I don't know!" Axel was unsettled, Amiel could see. She longed to press the argument, to attack while his foundations were shaking, but it was important that they worked together to reach Decius. She returned to the tiller, and left the youth to his thoughts.

Chapter Nineteen

"Why were the battlements on this side?"

"Excuse me?" Axel surfaced from a daydream at the boat's tiller. Amiel had been staring back into the mist, thinking about the reinforcements high on the side of the mountain.

"I've been thinking," she admitted to him. "A lot of things about this are strange. The gates were built to meet people as they travelled in the direction we are going. Why are those battlements on this side, looking out over the river? They would only see people leaving the gate, or other men under Decius travelling to them. Why not have a tower or walls on the other side?"

"Good point," Axel mused. He sounded thoughtful. His silence, however welcome it had been at first, had begun to unnerve Amiel. "But that place looked old, and it was cut really deep into that god-mountain. Maybe it has been there for a long time, for hundreds of years, and they just moved in there because it was a convenient place to fortify and the only way to pass those mountains safely. I mean, it was the ancients at the western end of the Empire who had all the myths about the gods and their mountains. It makes sense that the fortifications would point outward from their nation, according to their perspective,"

Amiel nodded. She hadn't thought of that. "Yes. The mountains might have formed the natural frontier of an empire on our side of the forest, long ago."

"Or that could have been an old temple or church," Axel offered. "It's in one of the god-mountains, after all."

Amiel considered that, but the building had seemed purely military to her. Plus, the ancients had believed the gods lived there because they were inaccessible, hostile and barren. They would not have had the same awe of the mountains' grim mystery if they had been running through tunnels within them like ants. Had it been fortified before or after the mountain became known as Justice? Had the fortress in its core been long abandoned when it was decreed that the double peak was the seat of a god? In its shadowy halls, Amiel had certainly felt the weight of centuries. She believed an even older people than those ancients from her frontier had fortified those ramparts. Long forgotten now.

She looked at Axel, but he had fallen silent once more, turned away from her. She knew the death of Gwydion was troubling him, and though, as a soldier, she didn't understand his disquiet, she knew she had to tackle it.

"Why did you need to fight him?" she asked quietly. At the tiller, Axel sighed. His head bowed briefly, then his eyes met hers once more and he began to speak.

"It's not like the stories," he began. "I'm not a fast-talking pickpocket from a great city. I don't live among the vermin and sleep in the gutters, part of an underground guild. I'm not a noble prince travelling the realm to understand his people better." He smiled weakly at her, "I'm not a street-thief who is a prince but doesn't know it, either."

Amiel knew all of this. Someone who lived and died on the dirty streets she had known would not be disturbed by killing someone. The street-thieves she could think of would have body counts in the double figures before breakfast. She knew he wasn't a noble, either. His accent marked him for a Northman, and although of course there were nobles up there, Axel didn't speak like them. His speech was too informal, his charm too easy-going when conversing with a soldier such as her.

"Truth to tell, my life was... normal," Axel told her. "My parents were both carpenters. Nothing from the storybook there either. We didn't live in grinding poverty. We had more than enough. We were happy. My father didn't drink or beat me; my mother didn't tell me I was worthless. They were really very kind. They did right by my brothers and I. But it wasn't enough for me. I wanted something *more*. I wanted excitement, I wanted adventure. I left home when I was thirteen."

"And what happened?" Amiel asked.

"I discovered 'adventurer' is not a paid job," Axel told her, his smile rueful. "There were no maidens to rescue or stolen treasures to retrieve. I drifted, wandered. I stole what I needed, avoided the bigger, nastier thieves. Got beaten up and robbed a few times. Eventually I learnt enough to fend them off and then run away. The thefts were hardly frequent though. Mostly, I just did odd jobs or begged. I just wanted to be safe while I was doing it."

"Explains your knife fighting skills," Amiel said. "Although I think there's a large amount of natural talent there as well."

"Praise from the soldier," Axel's smile became more genuine for a moment. "That's something. Thank you. Yes, I learnt knives were easy to conceal, and made people rethink fighting you quite quickly, whether you were robbing them or they were robbing you. But they're useless if you're just waving them around, so with the help of a few older friends I learned how to fight with one properly. But that... that was my first real fight. When you found me in the forest... I was running away but they surrounded me. Even then, I just injured that one man before you killed him. With Gwydion, I was trying to win, not just threaten him enough or disarm him or wound him so I could run away."

"Then why were you so desperate to fight him?"

"Well first of all, I underestimated him. The man was a lizard, but he could *fight*. Of course, that's what he wanted. I let myself be goaded, which was stupid. Most of all though, I wanted to play my part."

"What do you mean?" Amiel asked.

"Well this is it, isn't it?" Axel said. "This is a story. A grand adventure. Three heroes, a mission, an evil warlord for us to kill. Only it's too cold all the time, the mist is making me damp and no one can really agree on just *who* it is we are going to kill, other than the fact that he's bad. Oh, and I'm useless."

"What do you mean?"

"Next to you and Death's Left Hand over there?" Axel dropped his voice as he indicated Jenvilno at the prow, his face wry. "We've got a tough, seasoned soldier and a man so strong and so possibly insane he marched on an enemy fortress alone and with no armour."

Amiel almost bristled at this flippant insult to the saint, but she let it go.

"So next to that," Axel said, serious again, "I felt inadequate. I felt like an unnecessary part. Who can blame me? And so, when I saw a general who sounded like a pompous idiot and looked like an easy target, I went for him. Miraculously, I survived. But he died. I didn't want him to, no matter how obnoxious or bad he was. I'll try to find other ways to be useful from now on. I'll leave the fighting and killing to others. You can have this."

Axel took the knife sheath from his waist. Reaching out, he passed it to Amiel. She took the blade, and fastened it at her right hip, opposite her sword on the left.

"I'm sure you'll put it to better use than I would," Axel said.

Amiel smiled. She saw his hand on the tiller and patted it. "I still need you to hunt, at the very least."

"Oh yes? Would you starve without me?" Axel asked, sceptical.

"Undoubtedly. My skills are many and varied, but hunting is not one of them. Neither is cooking, actually."

"You managed to char that deer for us fairly

adequately," Axel said.

"Yes, well. That was an unusual piece of luck, I think. My normal specialty is both charred *and* raw."

"You mean charred outside, raw inside?"

"No," Amiel admitted. "I mean charred at one end and raw at the other."

Axel laughed, the sound loud and jarring over the silence of the river. He quickly stopped, muffled by the atmosphere around them, but still he smiled at her. Silence descended once again, but a comfortable one. Amiel watched Axel as he operated the tiller, thinking about what he had said. After a few moments, a question began to bother her and she spoke again.

"'Death's Left Hand'?"

"Well..." Axel sounded almost defensive, "what am I supposed to call him? Look at him, can you say it doesn't fit? It was that or the Man With No Face."

Amiel chuckled. "You are ridiculous," she told the boy. But she couldn't stop herself from smiling.

Chapter Twenty

The mist cleared enough to show the shores on either side. They were mostly bare, greyish mud interspersed with colourless patches of grass. Twisted, malnourished trees appeared here and there, but for the most part the ground was flat. This made sense to Amiel, if the mountains had in ages past formed a frontier barrier to a nation. The land would have been cleared of any sort of cover so approaching enemies could be seen. It would almost have been pleasant, free of the confines of the trees, but the surrounding fog formed a wall between them and the open sky, more oppressive even than the thick woods. Lost in this grey, her saint beside her, strange cries of animals echoing from the otherwise silent wilderness, Amiel felt she had passed into another world altogether, a dream-land of ancient rites and trials.

Axel spoke from the tiller, "tell me more of Janvier."

She turned to face him. She still scanned his face for mockery whenever he spoke, but now more often than not it was missing. "What would you like to know?"

"Why is he so popular where you are from? I haven't exactly travelled all over the Empire, but even three towns away from you he's barely a footnote. What is it that makes him the centre of the faith where you're from?"

Amiel glanced over at Jenvilno. He now sat near the prow of the boat. He still faced forward. She felt strange talking about the saint when he existed in the flesh so close to her, but he never seemed to be listening to anything. Beyond the few times he had spoken to her, he barely seemed to acknowledge the people around him. She wondered if she and Axel sounded like chattering animals to him, wondered if the distance between divine and human consciousness was as wide as that. At any rate, he paid no mind to their words.

"It's where he is from too," she said. "Saint Janvier lived there, over two thousand years ago. It's where he fought, where he performed his miracles, and where he died."

"I thought he was the fulfilment of a prophecy?" Axel said. "Isn't that how he sits in the boat with us now?"

"No," Amiel said. "It is as I said when I first realised who he was. He lived his first life back then, but it was always foretold he would return to end the evil of Deseme. Some think this means that he has never left us. That after the events we know of his life, he merely slept in a sacred cave or lived among us as a normal man until the time came for his final quest."

"You don't sound like you believe that," Axel said.

"I don't," Amiel admitted. "He is a saint, not a god. He lives by the rules of flesh. How could he live for two thousand years or sleep for so long? He would age or die of starvation. Plus, we know that he died a martyr. It is how he became a saint in the first place. No, he lived and he died then. I don't know how, but I believe when the time came, he was... reborn into the flesh, or sent back here somehow. It was the will of *Theos*, and now Janvier is among us."

"How did he die?" Axel asked.

"Janvier performed many miracles while he was alive, the power of *Theos* working through him. Arid lands he walked across would bloom with lily of the valley. Foul waters he touched would run clear. Diseases would vanish from the bodies of the afflicted. Armies he fought alongside would never lose. Animals would come to his outstretched hands. A golden light would shine from his eyes and brow, and *Theos* would work through him. He marched all over the land in his bright armour, protecting the weak and spreading the name of *Theos*.

Between his quests, he would live quietly in my town. He founded a church there, and served as the priest. He was praying there one day when they came for him."

"Who?" the boy asked.

"Armies from the far north, where the word of *Theos* had not been heard. No one knows just who they were, or who led them. Some say they come from beyond the cold northern seas, but that cannot be true. Their armour was dark, and their souls black. It is said they sacrificed to malicious spirits, not even really gods. These spirits took the forms of half-men hybrids, and ruled over small domains like battlefields and rivers where victims were ritualistically drowned. Janvier had walked among them years before, fought many of their greatest champions. When he defeated each one, he offered them a choice. Renounce their evil ways and take up the worship of the one true god... or die on his blade, their ends swift and merciful. He killed a great many. But there were always more of them, and this army of darkness swore revenge on him."

"What happened?" Axel kept his grip on the tiller, but listened raptly to her story.

"The savages tore their way into the church. They smashed the stained-glass windows, the ornaments and the holy relics. They tore the altar to pieces as Janvier knelt at it in prayer. Finally, the soldiers surrounded him. They demanded Janvier rise up, and face them in combat. Janvier looked at the army around him, and knew his life was over. No matter how many men he killed, the soldiers would eventually tear him to pieces. Janvier looked at each of the front rank in turn, and he refused to fight at all."

"He refused?"

"All his life, Janvier had fought for others. Defending the weak, defeating evil. He knew if he fought now, he would be fighting for himself alone, and so he refused. He looked them in the eyes, and he said he was ready

111

for *Theos* to judge him, for good or ill. The army murdered him, and where his blood flowed, white flowers grew. The dark army turned and marched north again. The townspeople had hidden when the soldiers came, and only now did they approach the church. They found the building demolished, its artefacts and glass broken, they found the body of the holy man. The soldiers had ripped him into nine pieces, but when they found him, he was miraculously whole, his flesh untouched. They gathered the shards of beautiful stained glass, and with them they made a holy necklace. They buried Janvier deep beneath his church, and rebuilt it over the ruins. They set a statue of the great knight above his own crypt, and on it they placed the necklace of sacred shards. When news of his death reached the Holy City at the centre of the Empire, he was instantly declared a saint for his works. We have loved him ever since."

"It's always strange, isn't it?" Axel asked.

"What is?" Amiel felt her defences rise.

"Well, in every religion, all the miraculous events happened a really long time ago, didn't they? I mean... flowers blooming, tame animals, magic healing... no one ever did that last week, did they? It's always thousands of years ago. I'm from the north, and it's the same with the old religions people used to worship there. You were right; they were these hunched, twisted little spirit-creatures who would live under an ancient battlefield or in the trunk of an old hanging tree, things like that. There would be lots of stories about them appearing on the night of a full moon, making deals with people and tricking them, kidnapping virgins or asking riddles. But all these stories supposedly happened long ago, just like your miracles. I'm no theologian, but I would think that if any one religion was right, you'd see it *happening*."

"Miracles still happen," Amiel said. "You hear about it all the time."

"Yes, but they're small miracles, and a bit dirty. Caught up in human concerns, down here with the grime and sweating bodies. Someone claiming to be miraculously cured, a weeping statue that could just have dew on it. You mentioned light shining from Janvier's head. When is the last time you saw that? When is the last time anyone saw a pillar of fire from the sky? Heard the disembodied voice of *Theos*? When did someone last return from the dead? Hundreds of years ago, at least. It's the same with every god."

"So, you don't believe in... anything?" Amiel asked, waiting for his scorn.

"No. But that doesn't make me right," Axel admitted. He turned his gaze on her. "Look, before, I was... rude. You and I think different things. I shouldn't have made fun of you. I can't hold to a belief system like you can, because of my doubts. You're clever, you must have the same doubts, and yet you keep faith. That takes guts. And whether I like it or not, you do keep predicting what will happen next. *Something* very strange is happening."

Amiel smiled gently. "Maybe we'll see a pillar of fire from the sky soon."

"Brilliant," Axel said. "Let's hope it's pretty close. Not close enough to burn us of course, just close enough so I can tell if I have hands and feet without looking."

"I was about to say you are much less of an idiot than I first thought, but now I'll just keep that to myself," she told him.

"Thanks, thanks," Axel said with a soft laugh. Silence fell between them, and he looked beyond her, into the mist. "Will you tell me our entire path, then? What awaits us?"

"Oh, no," Amiel said. "For the attitude you gave me about this, you can wait and find out about it stage by stage. We'll see how long you can keep denying it."

"Fine," he said. "That's not irritating or petty at all,

Amiel. Who is next, then?"

Amiel looked at the banks, something catching her eye. The trees were growing more and more frequent, hiding the grey mud, growing taller and thicker as the boat drifted forward.

"The next General," she told Axel, "is the Priest."

Mythmaking: Part Three

Janvier will next come to the church of the Priest. The Priest will agree to fight, but he will ask first that he and Janvier kneel together in prayer, that his god may look upon them with favour. Noble Janvier will bow his head, and together they will take to their knees. Together they will pray, and together they will ask only for an honourable fight and a blessing on their opponent's soul.

The prayers over, the fight will begin. The Priest will fight well, and his faith will be strong. But Janvier, and mighty Lux at his side, will prove stronger still.

The Priest, wounded by the great sword, will know his death is coming and accept it with grace. Even as he dies, he will say one more prayer for the soul of Janvier.

Janvier will lay the Priest out with great reverence and respect, and go on with his journey.

Chapter Twenty-One

For a long time, all that was above and around them was fog and the hidden sky. The sun shone in icy gold far beyond the mist, giving them no warmth. The trees began to crowd closer together, lining the bank and hiding it from view once more. The forest Gwydion had referenced gradually took hold of the land, until they were trapped beneath the green canopy. The trees crowded in thicker than before, boughs hanging low over the water as the boat whispered beneath them. The smell of damp vegetation was all around them, so strong the air felt almost liquid itself. Amiel saw Axel shivering.

"The Priest will give us shelter," she assured him.

"Nice sort, is he?" Axel said.

As ever, his lack of formality when talking about the myth around them annoyed Amiel, but she was glad in any case, he seemed to be at least halfway believing it now. This third gate would prove her right beyond all doubt. The noble and kind Priest would treat them well, and pray for their souls even in defeat.

"Amiel," Axel was looking over her shoulder. His eyes were wide, and though pale from the chill in the air, he was now almost white.

Amiel followed his gaze. A branch stretched low over the river, its wood dark and ancient. It had once been higher, but near the great bole of its tree, it was cracked. Wrapped in creeper, it danced and swayed in the soft breeze. A body hung from it, its neck in a noose. Where before the corpse had hung high, the cracking branch had brought it low, and now its feet trailed in the water. Keeping her eyes on it, Amiel grabbed the tiller from Axel, steering the boat to the left of the body and observing it as they passed. It was a man, but that was all she could tell. The flesh was withered, the body dead for long years, kept from rotting too badly by the cold air. Its feet were swollen where they dipped beneath the water's surface.

Amiel heard Axel's breath. It was too quick and shallow. Something was wrong. There were shadows over the water, up ahead. She wanted to slow their progress, to stop for the sake of the boy beside her. But the current was merciless and it only drew them forward, deeper into the dark tunnel of trees, further toward the shapes she could see above the water.

They were all bodies. Only some at first. Then dozens. Then more. As the boat drifted further forward, as they passed each group of corpses, more and more were waiting for them. All suspended from the branches, too numerous to count now. Some swung over the water, some from the branches at the banks. Straining her eyes, Amiel could see more, stretching further back into the forest. They swung gently at all heights. Every branch groaned under the weight of a body. Amiel turned to look back down the river, and bit back a shout as something brushed her shoulder. Leaving Axel to scramble for the tiller, she spun and lashed out with her sword, thrashing at the dead foot that had traced a gentle path along the side of her neck. This body was still fresh, bloated and stinking even in the cold air.

Then they were away from the body, leaving it to jerk and twist on its rope from Amiel's blow, its movement eerie among its motionless companions. Further they went, and still around them were hundreds of hanged men and women. Even when Amiel looked away, down at the dark water, she could still see the hanging bodies from below, reflected in its surface.

"What... what happened here?" Axel's face was drawn, as haunted as she was by the great gallows-trees all around them. She turned to look at him.

"It wasn't just one event," she told him. "It's still happening. Some of these bodies are almost fresh, some are ancient. Whoever did this is still active."

"Who?" Axel's voice was almost desperate. "Who could do this? Who could hang so many people?"

"There has to be more than one of them, working together," Amiel told him. "I stopped counting just past a hundred bodies, and that was right before that one touched me."

"Do you think... the Priest?" Axel faltered.

"He might know who did this." Amiel knew what he was asking. "When we find the next gate, we will ask what is happening here. And where we can find the killer."

"We're going to find the person who did this?" Axel asked.

Amiel nodded. "And hope he has a spare noose to hand."

She expected Axel to feel better at this, but the youth kept staring ahead, his eyes growing glassy. Amiel turned again, feeling slow, as if underwater. Facing forward, she saw what awaited them. She numbed herself to what she was seeing, faced it head on, did not flinch.

Jenvilno stood at the prow of the boat, unmoved from when the journey had begun. Past his lean figure, further down the river, Amiel could see two titanic trees with thick branches crossing high above the water. From their boughs, corpses hung so thickly that they formed a solid mass. Suspended on ropes of different lengths, they formed a huge arch shape, swinging and twisting subtly on their ropes. A gateway of dead flesh into the forest beyond. The current was pulling the boat along, into the mouth of the corpse-arch. Slowly, the boat slid through. Amiel looked upward into the hanging mass of the dead, wrapped in shadow. Nine corpses deep, the arch loomed around them. A hush descended on them. Even their breathing was almost silent. The only sounds Amiel could hear were the sluggish creak of ropes and the childlike cries of a carrion bird.

Was this even real? The forest was so quiet, everything was so strange. The mist everywhere, the corpses, the silence. Was this truly happening? Or was she having a vision, was the saint or *Theos* showing her what awaited further down the path? Both the god and his saints had epiphanic powers. But what future could a forest of hanged corpses signify? Amiel shook her head, looked again at the corpses arching over her, breathed in their decay, remembered the cold touch of the one she had struck. This was real, and she would find who did it.

The current was slow, but finally it took them through the corpse-arch and Amiel could draw breath again, the fresh air untainted by the dead. She gazed around in disgust and wonder. Beyond the archway, the forest opened out slightly, into a clearing. The canopy was thinner, and shafts of grey light struggled down through the leaves. Pale and peaceful in the half-light, the dead hung all around them. They filled even this vast space in the trees.

At the centre of the clearing, beneath the dome formed by the treetops, the river curved suddenly, snaking around the edge of a small hill. At the crown of this hill, a stone building towered toward the canopy. The building faced out across the river, so the travellers only saw the front as they drew level with it. It was a great church. Its stones were stained with moss and age. Its tower ended in a huge spire that almost stabbed into the leaves above it. Windows lined its walls, majestic and arched, filled with beautiful stained glass. Amiel was too far to see what they depicted, but she could feel their religious power. This was the next gate, the house of the Priest. So far from the centre of the Empire, and yet the hand of *Theos* reached even here. Inside they would pray, and they would fight.

But why were the corpses at their thickest here? Had the killer murdered the Priest, and taken the church for his lair? Amiel's eyes narrowed. If he had blasphemed in such a way, his inevitable death at her hands would be even more deserved.

Ahead of them, as the river curved around the church, they found their way blocked again. This time, the gate was made of thick ropes forming an impossible tangle across the water. Amiel took the mooring rope of their boat and splashed into the shallows. Finding a tree stump jutting from the earth, she tied the rope to it quickly and turned to wait for the others. Jenvilno vaulted from the boat, but barely made a ripple in the water as he landed. Axel followed more slowly,

"Do we have to go in? We could leave the boat, go overland from here. We could bypass the gate."

Amiel gestured at the edge of the clearing.

"And go through the forest? We would be lost within minutes."

"We could cut through those ropes," Axel offered. "We don't need someone to open that for us."

"Did you see how many ropes barred the path, and how thick they are?" Amiel countered. "It would take us days to cut through them. This is the only way."

She turned, and walked into the church.

Chapter Twenty-Two

More bodies awaited them inside the church.

They hung from the great wooden beams above. Their flesh was dry and withered, covered in ancient dust. The air hung heavy and stale, and the dead were motionless on their ropes.

The three stood at one end of a long, rectangular room. Along the walls to either side of them were many huge windows. Amiel looked at the first as they passed, and saw it filled with beautiful stained glass. The pale light from outside struck the glass and made it glow, and she paused to study the illuminated scene.

In the centre was a slender figure with white hair. His lower half was clad in armour, but from the waist up he was naked. He hung in mid-air, his face slightly upturned and smiling serenely, his eyes closed. His feet were together but his arms were outstretched. Behind his head a halo of golden light burned, and his whole body gave off its own, softer glow. To either side of him thronged crowds of people, kneeling before his light. Amiel looked carefully at this gathering, confused. To the left of the figure, the people kneeling had smiles of their own. They reached for the glowing man before them, their eyes shining with ecstasy as they strove to touch his outstretched hand, his legs, and the end of a deep red sash trailing from his waist. To the right, the kneeling people recoiled from the shining man in terror. Their faces were contorted with fear or pain, and they clamoured to crawl away from him. Amiel took a step toward the glass. Looking closer, she saw that some of the faces on the left were filled with that same terror, and some of those on the right showed blissful reverence. And with some of the expressions, it was hard to tell.

Who was this? She knew of no saint who appeared this way, no man who inspired love and fear in equal measure. She knew most of the saints and martyrs of *Theos*, but it was possible that this one, so far beyond the last frontier of the Empire, had been forgotten long ago. Perhaps those in fear were heretics? Sinners? It was impossible to say.

Confused and haunted by the image, she walked on, behind Axel and Jenvilno.

As she strode through the body of the church, she looked to her left and her right, glancing at the other glowing stained-glass windows. She saw a great tree, dark and twisted. She saw the same white-haired man, surrounded by shadowy figures and she couldn't tell if the expression on his face was a laugh or a scream as they reached for him. She saw a large, dark building rising against a stormy sky and she saw the noose. Everywhere, she saw the symbol of the noose. It decorated the corners of the stained-glass windows; it was carved into the wooden beams and set in the stone of the walls. Amiel looked from these nooses to the hanging corpses all around them and shuddered. Had the murderer of all these people merely been inspired by the symbol carved throughout the church, or was this a relic from some ancient sect? Some darker, older saint who demanded veneration by human sacrifice? Was it even a church of *Theos* at all, or was this the seat of some savage, primal god long forgotten? Maybe this was the house of one of the dead gods of the wind-blasted mountains they had passed under.

The three walked between two rows of pews, picking their way around those bodies suspended in their path. Amiel looked at the seats and saw again the symbol of the noose, cut into their dark wood. She almost walked into Axel's back before she realised that he and Jenvilno had stopped. They had reached the front of the church.

This entire end of the building was taken up by a vast altar, hewn from pale stone. Flanked by unlit candles, it rose to the ceiling of the towering church, adorned all over with plates of gold. At the top, it showed again the great and twisted tree, beaten into the metal. At the centre of the altar was a huge alcove, rising up and crowned by an arch. Standing in this was a mighty statue, looking down over the church. Amiel looked upon it, and knew it showed the same white-haired man from the stained-glass windows. He wore no clothing, and posed as if in mid-step. His left arm was outstretched, reaching down toward the empty benches. His right was held out to one side, raised slightly, grasping a rope which ended in a noose around his neck. In the altar's hollow, his face was in shadow, but Amiel saw the hint of a smile on his lips.

Before the altar was a huge wooden chair. Carved from the same dark wood as the pews, it sat on four thick legs. Its back flared upward, fashioned into a mysterious pattern Amiel couldn't see well enough to study. Against it lay a silver staff, its top crowned with the merciless loop of a noose, the coils of the rope fashioned into the metal. But she wasn't looking at the chair, none of them were. Above it hung the corpse of an old man.

He wore soiled robes of white, edged with silver. His feet, bound with strips of silver cloth, swung slightly, inches above the seat of the great chair. His face was covered by a beard that had once been white but was lank now, stained with filth. It trickled down onto his chin, which sunk forward to rest on the noose suspending him. His shoulder-length hair was dirty too, cut unevenly by an uncaring hand.

"Where is the general?" Axel's voice, though only a murmur, startled Amiel in the stillness of the church. She turned to look at him, and saw the eerie church had unnerved him as much as it had her.

"Everyone here is dead. Where is he?" he asked again.

"I... I don't know," Amiel confessed. She stared at the corpse above the chair, trying to find words and failing. Silence descended once more in the dust-coated belly of the church. For a second only, Amiel felt lost. Then she spun on her heel and began to walk.

"Come on," she snapped. "You were right; we'll have to cut through those ropes."

Axel turned too and began to follow her. But Jenvilno didn't. The masked warrior remained motionless, staring at the corpse above the chair. Realising he was not with them, Amiel stopped and looked back. And so, she too saw the corpse begin to move.

Twitching, insect-like, the old man's dangling arms jerked into life and began to rise above his head. Spasms shook his hands as he reached, and his joints cracked, but eventually he grasped the rope above him in one fist. Something glinted in his other hand, gripped between finger and thumb. Amiel saw it was a broken piece of stained glass an instant before he sliced through the rope. The noose still around his neck, a length of rope trailing from it, the old man landed lightly on the great seat beneath him. With a slow step, he descended from the chair to the stone floor. The collar of his robe shifted as he climbed down, and for an instant Amiel saw something at his neck, beneath the noose. It looked to be a band of dark metal, but at that moment the old man adjusted his robe, and it was hidden beneath the cloth. If it was an iron collar, it would stop him from strangling on the end of his rope for a time, but still the pain would be great. What sort of man would subject himself to that?

The fragment of glass fell from his fingers, rang softly against the ground where it dropped. His hand snaked out and took the silver staff from beside the chair. Gripping it at the middle, he began to walk toward them. The tip of the staff trailed along the stone floor, and Amiel saw that it ended in a jagged blade. Barbed and cruel, it hissed against the stones. The old man stopped before them, his face unreadable, watery eyes staring at them from beneath matted brows.

His voice was hoarse, rasping from long misuse, but the one word his lips formed was clear enough.

"Challengers?"

Amiel nodded. At this movement the old man's head snapped sideways with a jerk, his eyes resting on her.

"Yes," she answered. "Are you the general?"

"I am," his voice became clearer the more he spoke. "I am the Priest."

"Was it you who did this?" Axel was struggling to keep his voice even. Amiel forced herself to accept the unpleasant suspicion she had been avoiding as Axel spoke. She watched as he gestured to the other corpses, hanging all around them. "All of this?"

"Of course," the Hanging Priest showed no remorse. He showed no emotion at all. "I took them all and I hanged them high. Challengers, some of them. Others just lost and alone. Their souls cried out to me, begged to dance on the holy rope."

"Why? Why hang them?" A feverish light was in Axel's eyes, and Amiel laid a gentle hand on his arm to calm him.

The Priest blinked his faded eyes.

"Why...? As sacrifices, of course. Offerings to the great god Decius."

Chapter Twenty-Three

Amiel was the first to speak, but she could barely force the words out.

"The great god... Decius?"

"Yes," the Priest replied, a beatific smile slowly spreading across his face. "Stay and listen, and I shall tell you about the god you seek."

The Hanging Priest drew himself up, standing tall for the first time. He stood taller even than Jenvilno. His arms spread slightly to either side of him, one hand still gripping his staff. The Priest began his sermon.

"Decius was born into this world, a kind and benevolent god. Light was his domain, and truth. He walked among the people in kindness and harmony, and they loved him. It was a golden age, and the whole world knew only peace and happiness." As he spoke, his voice gaining strength with each word, the Priest's eyes rested on each of them in turn. "But it could not last. The other gods saw the love that the people had for Decius, and terrible was their envy, and the anger that came from it."

A tear glistened in the corner of the Priest's eye as he continued to speak, his voice shaking.

"They came upon Decius in his sacred grove. Do you understand? His *sacred grove*. Evil, jealous gods! They took him and they hanged him from the branch of a great tree. They hanged him by his neck and the god... the beloved god died."

The tremble left his voice, and a smile returned to the Priest's cracked lips. "But they failed. Greater still was the love of the people for Decius and through this love, or perhaps through the great power of the god alone, he returned to life. He returned to life and walked among the people once more, his neck forever marked by the rope that killed him."

The Priest leaned forward, his voice dropping as his smile became a grin, a leer. "But death changed Decius. Reborn, he was violent now, and cruel. He became the Lord of Lies and Pain, and great was the pestilence he spread across the world. For who better to rule lies than he who owns the truth? And what hurts more than the burning of divine light?"

His teeth remained bared, but the smile slithered from his face.

"Those who were faithful, the true believers, loved Decius nonetheless. If he wishes to bring suffering to us, who are we to question it? Is it not his right as a god, as something far above human, to do what he wishes? But not all of us held to our faith. There were those among the people who decided they had endured enough, that it was *their* duty to decide when their pain ended, and not the right of the one true *god*."

The Priest looked now at Amiel, and his eyes chilled her. "Blasphemers. They banished the god, Decius. They banished him with charms and black prayers. They sealed him far beyond us, in his great cathedral. Deep within its hollow halls he waits, chipping away at the power that seals him there. He waits and he gathers his strength, and in time he will break free. He will return to the world to save it or, depending on which side of him is now dominant, to end it."

He relaxed, and his smile became peaceful once more. "And so, I hang here in honour of my god. I wait for his return, whether he brings with him blessing or burning. At the end of my rope, I wait. All who pass through here must face me, both the good men who wish to pay their respects at the cathedral... and the evil men, the servants of hell, who seek to break in and murder the great god Decius before he can return. Hundreds I have fought, and hundreds I have hanged. So many bodies hoisted high. Dedicated to Decius, my devotion to him."

The Hanging Priest gripped his staff now in both hands, planted the blade on the floor at his feet. Holding it before him, staring at them through the staff's symbolic noose, he spoke. "I ask you now, which one of you will face me? Which one of you will fight?"

Amiel's voice disturbed the dead air in reply.

"He will." She gestured at the masked man next to her, "Jenvilno will fight you."

Without a word, Jenvilno stepped forward. His boots scraped along the stone as he moved to stand before the Priest. With a whisper, loud as a shriek in the still church, he drew his sword. The Priest nodded.

"Yes, yes," he smiled. "You have the look of a true warrior. Decius will be most pleased with you. Come, kneel with me, and together we will pray to the Great God."

Silence fell on the church once more. The seconds lengthened. Dust, disturbed by the noise in the long-silent hall, slid from where it had lain for long years and swirled through the air. The Priest stared at Jenvilno, and behind his mask the fighter's grey eyes were unblinking.

"No," he answered at last.

Chapter Twenty-Four

The Priest's saintly smile drained from his face. His voice was soft when he spoke.

"Then I name you Jenvilno *Theomachos*, who fights against god. I name you Jenvilno Heretic, and Jenvilno Adversary. I will hang you high, and you will die outside of the light. It is time. Prepare yourself."

He raised his staff and reversed it, the blade pointing at the masked warrior. Jenvilno's hand tightened around his sword, and slowly he turned, taking his fighting stance.

With a shout, the Priest lunged. Amiel hid her reaction, not wanting Axel to know, but she was astonished. Though he was an old man, and though he hanged himself by the neck in his deranged worship, the Priest attacked with unbelievable speed. The blade of his staff hissed through dust as it whipped toward Jenvilno's throat. Gwydion had seemed fast, but Amiel knew the red-haired lord was nothing compared to the power of this general. Gwydion had fallen fighting Axel. Amiel looked across at the youth. She knew he realised as she did that only Jenvilno could stand against this strange, deadly old man. The blade of the staff hunted for the masked fighter's throat, but Jenvilno brought his shining sword up and blocked the attack. Metal rang against metal, and Jenvilno's boot ground in the accumulated dust of unknown years as he shifted his stance to keep balance.

Amiel looked at the masked warrior. He hadn't stumbled at the impact, but he had come close. Her face darkened as she watched the combatants. This was going to be a hard fight, she told herself, even for Jenvilno.

Behind the mask, the grey eyes narrowed slightly.

And then Jenvilno began. He hurled himself forward at the Priest, his blade rising, slicing through beams of pale light as it fell toward his opponent. Metal clashed again as the Priest defended, using the middle of the silver staff to deflect the masked warrior's blow. With a wolf-like grin, the Priest saw his chance. He shifted his grip on the staff and drove the blade end forward. Jenvilno dodged, but not fully. The blade plunged through his black jacket at the shoulder, and Amiel heard the hissing intake of breath behind the mask as the Priest's weapon found flesh. Jenvilno leapt back and began to circle. His left arm moved a little slower now, and behind the ripped cloth thin trickles of blood began to weep from his broken skin. He spared a glance at his injury, clenching his fist a few times, and then returned his frosty eyes to the Priest. Amiel let out a breath she seemed to have been holding forever. Only a minor injury, then. But still first blood had gone to their opponent, and it was with trepidation she watched the fight continue. The Priest tried to hold to his smile, but Amiel could hear anger infecting his words when he spoke.

"You won't fool me, Heretic. I know your true blood runs black. I'll just have to cut *deeper*!" His voice dropped to a snarl as he gripped his staff like a spear and rammed it at the masked fighter.

This time, Jenvilno was too fast. He darted around the slashing weapon, the blade inches from his side. The Priest tried to bring his staff in to defend but it was too ungainly in close quarters. Jenvilno lashed a murderous cut at the Priest's neck. The Priest managed to bring his staff up to block, but only succeeded in deflecting the blade against his face. Amiel felt Axel tense beside her as Jenvilno's sword gouged the Priest's flesh, from beneath his right eye to the left side of his jaw, taking part of the nose and tearing into his lips as it went.

The Priest stumbled back as blood began to well from the gash. It ran through his lank whiskers, staining his face and shoulders as it dripped, crimson on silver. Breathing heavily, he looked at Amiel and Axel with hollow eyes, torn mouth hanging loose. Serene beneath the horrible wound, his mutilated lips smiled. He held the staff in one hand. The other journeyed up to his ruined face. With one finger he probed the ripped skin and then, opening his mouth, the Priest licked fresh blood from his calloused fingertip and filthy nail.

"Pain," he said, smiling his dreamlike smile at Amiel. His words were mangled now. "Pain is good. It brings me closer to the god."

He turned again to Jenvilno, forgetting the blood seeping from his face as his smile widened.

"Let me show you."

He attacked.

Jenvilno ducked beneath the blade end of the staff. His sword flashed up in a disembowelling cut, but he opened a tear only in the Priest's billowing robes. The Priest attacked now with the heavy noose end of the staff. Jenvilno threw up an arm up to block the blow and it clubbed against his injured shoulder. As the Priest attempted to dart backward and gain some space, Jenvilno remained on the hunt. He smashed the staff aside with his sword hand, while his free hand grabbed for something. Amiel only realised what he was doing when the masked warrior's hand seized the trailing end of the noose around the Priest's neck. Dragging on the rope, Jenvilno hauled the Priest forward into a devastating punch from the fist closed around his sword hilt. Before he could deliver the killing blow with the blade, the Priest managed to scramble away. He crouched on the stone floor, dripping blood to mix with the dust. Slowly, he rose to his feet.

Jenvilno's punch had broken something in his face. The Priest's words were a slippery, grinding snarl now, distorted by pain and the damage to his lips and the bones behind them.

"You have a devil's strength, I will grant you. But Decius is within me, and my *faith will conquer*!"

As the wounded Priest spoke, voice rising to a scream, he raised his bladed staff for the final time. Stabbing at the air in his rage, he threw himself into the fight once more. The blade lanced downward, glinting in the weak light as it sought the masked killer. Jenvilno stepped away from it. The blade clattered against the floor, striking sparks from the stones. As the Priest cursed and struggled to lift it, Jenvilno stepped in close, around and away from the weapon. With his empty hand he drove another brutal punch into the Priest's face and, as his opponent staggered, the masked man's sword-arm drew back, slashed upward and across. Staggering, off-balance, the Priest couldn't defend as the blade of *Lux* ripped into his forearm, opening a long cut. The damage was serious, and the Priest's arm immediately fell useless to his side. The old man screamed as blood began to turn his silver robe red at the arm. His other hand still gripped the staff, but he was far too slow now, too damaged. He was only prey to the killer in the mask.

Jenvilno reversed his swing, never wasting a spare movement. Gripping the shining sword in two hands, he brought it hacking downward. The Priest screamed as the metal bit deep into his shoulder, snapping through bone. His terrible cry tore through the church again as Jenvilno dragged the blade clear. His functioning hand clutched the staff in a desperate grip, and the Priest fell to his knees.

Stepping forward, the masked warrior kicked the staff from his opponent's hand. The weapon smashed against a wooden pew and fell to the floor. Silent now, his breathing ragged, blood spurting from his wounds, the Priest looked up into the cold eyes behind the mask. He coughed, spat blood onto his killer's boots.

"Do it then." His voice was growing weaker, but the venom remained. "Kill me. Do you think it will make a difference? Those who fight against god can never know peace or rest. They can never know an end to their pain. So, strike, murderer. Strike, monster. Strike, *Jenvilno.*"

Something cold moved in Amiel when she saw the eyes behind the mask. Jenvilno stared down at the Priest. The old man stared back, defiant. For several heartbeats the two were motionless. Axel recoiled next to her, and Amiel strangled a cry in her throat as Jenvilno exploded into terrible life. He reversed his grip on *Lux*, the glowing blade pointing downward. He lifted it high in both hands, his back arching with the force, and then he plunged down into the Priest's injured shoulder. He struck even harder this time, and the blade burrowed into the Priest's chest. The old man made no sound as he died. His final breath rattled from him and his eyes lost their light. Jenvilno placed a boot on his victim's chest, and dragged his blade clear. The corpse collapsed backward to rest in the dust. Wordless, Jenvilno looked down at the body. Silent moments drifted by.

He turned, and walked from the church.

Chapter Twenty-Five

Outside, the web of ropes crossing the river had vanished. Amiel looked around in the silence of the clearing, unsettled. Who had taken the ropes? Did the Priest have accomplices who still lived, and were they watching now?

She set her jaw. It didn't matter. Only their mission mattered, and it was time to move on. Amiel walked toward the boat. She paused to untie the moorings, and the other two climbed into the vessel ahead of her. Fumbling with the ropes, she watched Jenvilno take his place at the prow. The boat free, and beginning to drift in the sluggish current, Amiel quickly leapt over the side. She steadied herself as the boat began to pick up speed, its sail finding a breeze somewhere in the forest's quiet air. The current, slow at first, rapidly picked up pace. It almost seemed something was dragging the boat forward.

Ahead of them, another opening in the trees beckoned, the green giving way to darkness within. With their last trip through the forest fresh in her mind, Amiel prepared herself for more grotesque sights, but these trees beyond the realm of the Priest were mercifully free of bodies. Axel had taken the rudder, so Amiel settled back on a wooden bench and tried to rest. Against her will, her eyes were drawn to Jenvilno. The warrior sat at the prow, staring into the mist, motionless once more. Once again, he was a silent statue of flesh, but Amiel knew now the fury and violence he was capable of. Again, and again she saw the end to the fight. The Priest's defiance, the brutal killing blow.

Was this truly Janvier? The thought was in her mind before she could prepare to ignore it. Janvier was noble, his quest virtuous. There was no place in his heart for rage. Why had she seen cold madness flash in the masked man's eyes in the instant before he struck? The thought sparked a fire in her mind, spreading outward. Why was everything happening differently to the myth's description? Why was everything twisted and distorted, or else completely wrong? Was it all truly happening, or was her faith misplaced? Was it the right thing to hunt this Decius?

That, she held in no doubt. They had heard he was a mad king, they had heard he was a bandit lord. That madman had even said he was a god. No matter what he was, anyone who would recruit someone like that murderous Priest was evil. Anyone who would knowingly join forces with that zealot deserved to be punished.

No, she told herself. Not punished. Neutralised. It did no good to think of law and justice. Everyone thought what they did was right and just, it was all a matter of perspective. The Priest had thought his bloodthirsty worship was right. Axel thought stealing from Decius was right. The man in the city to the east, the man she had killed before his children, had thought killing soldiers of the empire and disrupting the peace was a noble blow struck against conquerors. Her eyes closed as the man, the mission she tried not to think of, came into her mind's eye in sharp detail. He had needed to die, but she should have dragged him from the house when she realised his children were there. They had heard him die, and the thought of what they went through stirred unwelcome memories in her. Axel had said killing them would have marked her soul. He was right, but it had already been tainted by what she had done. Morals and justice. She had no right to speak of them. But this new mission was right. There was no question in her heart. The evil of Decius was to be removed from the world, to stop him doing any further damage to those around him; if he was as evil in reality as the myth painted him. This returned her to her original, uncomfortable thought process. Doubts swarmed her.

"What's next?" The voice cut through her thoughts. Amiel turned and saw Axel looking at her. His voice was soft, his face pale. The eyes that looked at her were exhausted and haunted, but earnest. "He wasn't playing a game, Amiel. He didn't just hear a story and decide to act it out for us. He lived it, hanging from that noose, killing all those people. He died for it. He *believed*, Amiel."

A weary smile split Amiel's lips. "So, you believe now as well?"

"It's not happening like you said it would. It's darker and dirtier and more violent but... maybe the stories can ignore all of that in the telling. Maybe this is the way it *has* to happen, in the real world."

Amiel reached out and took the hand that didn't rest on the boat's rudder. Axel squeezed her fingers and tried to smile back at her.

"What's next, Amiel?" he asked again. The smile slipped from her mouth. Her face darkened as she thought of the next gate, and what awaited them there. Steeling herself, she looked Axel full in the face as she gave her answer.

"The Savage. The Savage is next and... I'm afraid, Axel."

She saw the impact of her honesty in the young man's face. He almost recoiled, as if from a blow.

"You're..." he faltered, unable to finish. Amiel nodded.

"The Savage is a monster. Sadistic and murderous. When we step into his realm, we will pass through victorious, or we will suffer the fate of all of his victims."

"What does he do?" Axel's voice trembled. "What will happen to us?"

Amiel shook her head. He was frightened enough without knowing the atrocities awaiting them if they failed. She gazed again at the masked fighter's back as he sat at the prow. She thought of the next part of the myth, of the Savage tamed.

"We have to trust in his strength," she said to Axel. The youth was still frightened, but Amiel saw him swallow his fear in front of her, trying to be brave.

"I don't think anyone is stronger," he told her. "What was that word the Priest used, when Jenvilno wouldn't pray with him? Themolachos or something?"

"*Theomachos,*" Amiel corrected. "These days it means an unbeliever, who denies *Theos*. It's from a very ancient tongue, though. It literally means someone who makes war on a god."

"Are we doing that?" Axel asked.

"No," Amiel answered. "There is no god but *Theos*. Decius is the Mad King. That is what the myth says, it is what will be. Gwydion and the Priest may have told us different. But do you trust a liar and a madman?"

"So, you think that although some details are changing from the myth, more and more as we go on, the ultimate ending will remain the same?"

"Yes," Amiel answered with a surety she almost felt. "Janvier will sail up the river and defeat the Mad King Deseme. He will pass all of the gates and defeat all of the generals. None of that can change."

"I still don't know why he puts himself at such a disadvantage." Axel was staring now at Jenvilno, his dark clothing almost black against the mist they sailed into. "It's not just the lack of armour. It's the sword. That's not a sword for one-to-one duelling, is it?"

"No," Amiel conceded, revisiting her earlier thoughts on the weapon. "It's an infantry blade, like you said before. A gladius. Designed for close-quarters stabbing in a pitched battle, shoulder-to-shoulder with other heavily armoured troops. Not designed for sword-fights, or for hacking with the edge at all."

"Why use it, then?" Axel asked. "He's clearly an

incredible swordsman. The instinct he has, along with that speed and power. It's frightening. Why not use a longer sword like yours and shred insane old zealots in seconds?"

It was a good question, and one Amiel had considered herself, especially as the myth mentioned Janvier's shining armour and great helm, along with *Lux* itself. But then, she realised, that was the answer.

"The sword," she said to Axel. "Have you not seen the way it glows yet? I know you didn't think it was... before..." she trailed off.

"Before I knew something exceptionally strange was happening around us, yes." Axel thought about her question. "It certainly looks eerie, the way it catches the light. I thought that was all it was... but now I'm not certain."

"It is *Lux,* the sword of Janvier," Amiel told him. "It is the one *Theos* forged for him, and the one he must use for his final quest. Perhaps *Theos* wants to test his greatest saint, sending him out into the wilderness with no armour and a shortsword."

"Maybe," Axel said. "But after he fought those silent guards with his fists, and after the way he killed the Priest... do you not worry that he wants to be close to them? That he... enjoys it?"

"No," Amiel's voice was firm now. "He doesn't enjoy killing. He knows that our mission needs to be completed, and those in the way must be removed. He seems not to care about who he has to kill, but I know he regrets the necessity."

"I hope so," Axel said. "Because sometimes he *does* seem indifferent to it. Completely indifferent to it. And sometimes it frightens me."

Chapter Twenty-Six

Night fell, and as the skies turned from grey to black once more, the water began to grow shallow.

At first, Amiel thought their slowed progress was her imagination. Then she saw the weeds choking the water around them. She looked to Axel at the rear of the boat. The boy struggled and swore as he tried to tear the rudder free of the weeds. He looked up and their eyes met as, with a gentle, scraping impact, the prow of the boat struck a submerged sandbank. Axel released the tiller with a sigh. They both knew it was pointless now. The way was impassable. He looked a question at Amiel, but as she turned to check the river ahead of them, she saw the saint making ready to disembark. He took his sword-belt from his waist, refastening it so the short blade hung diagonally across his back. His eyes flashed in Amiel's direction as he leapt from the boat into the water. Submerged to his thighs, he struggled through the thick weeds toward the left bank. Amiel followed his progress, and saw a path cutting through the dense trees at the edge of the river.

So, they must continue on foot. So be it.

"Let's go," she ordered Axel. Unbuckling her own sword belt and holding it over her head, knowing the longer blade would slow her progress amongst the weeds even further. She vaulted over the side and into the river. The water reached close to her waist, and she bit back curses of her own as the plant life grabbed at her ankles. The small, dark shapes of alien fish scattered before her as she followed Jenvilno. She listened, and continued without slowing when she heard Axel gasping behind her. The bank was raised slightly, and she threw her sword to dry land before she climbed out. Turning, she seized Axel's arm and dragged him from the water.

Grabbing her blade from the ground, she gestured him to follow, and they set off into the trees behind the already vague form of the masked fighter.

In the dark of the forest once more, among unfamiliar sounds, Amiel kept her hand close to her sword-hilt. She thought back to when she had first entered the trees; a matter of days ago now, but it already seemed like impossible years ago. How long had it been, exactly? Amiel found she had no idea. Events fought and grappled with one another in her mind, one following the other with no seeming connection or order. The men of Decius, Jotun, Axel, Gwydion, the faceless guards, Gwydion's courtiers whose faces she could no longer remember, the Hanging Priest... and Jenvilno. At the centre of everything, binding every memory together.

"The path seems awfully clear, for a forest trail."

Axel's voice was soft beside her, and she didn't start. She looked at him, then down at the surface, feeling for the first time how hard and even it was. It shouldn't have been. It felt less like a forest path and more like the remnants of -

"A road," she breathed. "Are we reaching the next gate?"

"I don't think so," Axel said. He pointed ahead of them, to a structure almost lost in the trees at the side. "It's better-constructed than a forest path, but it hasn't been used in a long time. And what's that?"

"A waygate." Amiel answered before she knew she possessed the knowledge. "In the very first days of the Empire, structures like that marked the approach to smaller towns. A guard would be posted there, mostly to warn of approaching strangers. They fell out of use once the towns started growing bigger, and the fortifications more secure."

"In the very first days of the Empire?" Axel asked, "Then shouldn't that be far, far to the east of here?"

Amiel didn't answer. She had considered it herself. Why *was* an eastern-style waygate so far out here? Who had manned it? It was ruined, but not ancient. What had been here?

They drew level with it, and then passed the structure. Amiel was so engrossed in it that she almost didn't hear Axel's intake of breath, nor see the thinning trees in the growing darkness. She looked ahead, and almost cursed herself. Hadn't she just told the boy that waygates marked the approach to towns? She should have expected this.

Following Jenvilno, she and Axel walked into the ruined town.

Chapter Twenty-Seven

Even in the gathering dark, she could see the buildings had been burnt.

The richer-looking stone buildings were merely shells, and the far more common wooden ones had been gutted entirely and collapsed. An army had raged through the nameless town, destroyed it utterly, and the ground was still churned by the marks of their boots. How long ago it had happened, it was impossible for Amiel to tell. She had seen dozens of ruined towns, from ancient settlements long deserted to enemy cities or rebellious strongholds razed by the armies of *Theos* years or months or weeks before. The darkness, however, stopped her from properly examining the broken buildings and the ground to learn how long this town had stood empty.

"The Savage did this," Axel said to her left. It was not a question. She nodded, staring into the gloom. It was a cloudy night, and only sparse moonlight reached them. Just enough for her to pick a path through the town, enough to catch glimpses of the masked saint walking ahead. He did not pause, looking neither left nor right at the structures he passed. But his pace was not the punishing march he usually set, and Amiel joined Axel in loitering a little and looking at the ruins. Burned fifty years ago or just days before they had arrived, it was impossible for her to see. But one odd aspect stood out to her, made her think it must have been long ago.

"No bodies," she muttered. She couldn't see his face as it turned to her, but she guessed Axel was looking a question at her. She took a breath.

"It was clearly burned, sacked, at some time in the past. Even if the vast majority of inhabitants were taken, to be sold into slavery or killed elsewhere... even if they were taken, we'd still see some around here. Left where they fell. Where are the bodies?"

She expected no answer, and she received none from the boy. They walked through the silent town, past larger buildings as they neared the centre. Government buildings, military, judicial... whatever they had been, they no longer were. Time passed, and they reached the suburbs again, such as they were in a small settlement like this. As they neared its borders, a wide expanse of empty ground greeted them. Towering behind it, indistinct under the weak moonlight, was a rock face. It rose higher than the trees, the edge of a plateau or the scar of a forgotten cataclysm.

At its foot, extending almost to the edge of the town they now left, Amiel found the answer to one of her questions. Here were the town's lost occupants. The cliff face curved in a vast arc, lost to the shadows and swirling mist when she looked left or right. The ground before it was a massive graveyard, bathed in fog. The markers were simple. Wooden stakes, rammed into the ground. Vegetation growth was minimal, suggesting a recent burial, but when she got close enough to examine the nearest markers, she saw them inscribed with yet more ancient runes. Around the plants and grave markers, strange insects silently flitted in swift patterns, their bodies giving off otherworldly light in brief flashes.

"Here are the townspeople," she told Axel. "Buried after the Savage killed them."

"Buried by him, or his men?" he asked.

"Neither. He would have left the bodies to rot, and ordered his men to do the same. The survivors must have come back to bury their dead, before they moved on."

Her own words sounded convincing to her, but with the saint's final quest unfolding more and more strangely as they moved further into the forest, she couldn't be sure she was right. She couldn't be sure anyone had survived the rampage of the next general. A path ran between the graves, leading to the cliff face. Jenvilno strode down it, paying no more heed to the dead than he had to the broken town. Amiel followed him, expecting a tunnel at the base of the cliff.

As they drew closer and she saw that only solid rock awaited them, she knew their path ended there. They joined the motionless saint at the cliff.

"What now?" Axel's voice was quiet. He had been shaken by his killing of Gwydion, and their encounter with the Priest had changed him entirely. Amiel almost missed his mockery, missed his lopsided grin. She was at a loss. The way was blocked, and she didn't know where else to go. She cast her gaze upwards, her eyes catching on five objects at the top of the high cliff.

She pointed upward, "What are they?"

Axel strained his eyes, squinting through the mist as he followed her hand.

"I don't know," he said eventually. "They look like... stakes?" He nodded as he spoke, growing surer as the words left his mouth. "Stakes, with something on top of them."

Amiel looked again. He was right. It looked like five stakes jutting from the lip of the cliff, with round objects stuck on top of them. She began to shudder.

"Are they..." she began.

"Skulls?" Axel finished for her, voicing her fears. "I think so."

Without warning, Jenvilno started forward again. His sword still strapped to his back, he approached the cliff.

"What is he doing?" Axel asked.

"He's right," Amiel murmured. "The skulls were set there as a warning. That's the way to the gate of the Savage."

Chapter Twenty-Eight

Amiel watched the masked fighter reach the face of the cliff. One hand flashed out and upward, his fingers hooking around a handhold in the rock. Jenvilno began to climb. Axel turned to Amiel, a weak smile on his lips.

"I don't suppose there's some sort of Bloodthirsty Staircase around the corner?" he asked.

Amiel saw the strain in this pale reflection of the Axel she had known before the church, before the death of Gwydion. She wanted to reassure him, but her nerves were growing as they neared the gate, and her reply was curt as she checked and re-secured her own sword on her back.

"Afraid not. We'll have to climb."

"I thought so." Axel shook his head, but followed Amiel to the cliff face. Closer to it, Amiel saw that the rock was caked with mud and loose vegetation, slippery and treacherous. Steeling herself, she reached out and took the first handhold. Behind her, Axel pressed his hat more firmly onto his head and prepared to follow her.

The cliff face was scarred from centuries of wind and water, and the rock presented many handholds for Amiel as she climbed. But the way was long, and soon her arms ached and her muscles trembled. She looked up, and saw the edge of the cliff, mocking them from far above. Beneath her, Axel followed the path she set. She did not dare to look down, but from his breathing she knew that the climb was eating at his strength too. Clouds of the glowing insects flitted in circles around her head, and Amiel angrily brushed at them with her hand, failing to drive them away. Suddenly larger, darker shapes were fluttering around her, black wings striking her face as she clung to the cliff. Her eyes narrowed to slits, one hand releasing its hold to shield her face, Amiel saw small bats darting in and out of the holes in the cliff where they roosted. They snapped after the glowing insects, needle-like teeth snatching the shining bodies from the air. Ignoring them, Amiel resumed her climb. She didn't look up now, and still feared to look down. She looked only for her next handhold, her face pressed tight to the dirty stone of the cliff. After an unknown length of time, minutes or seconds or hours of staring at the rock with pain in her muscles, a noise from above reached Amiel. She looked up in time to see Jenvilno disappear over the top of the cliff, now much closer. Despite the agony in her arms, despite the strange events behind them and awaiting them, she sighed with relief. The climb was nearly over.

She saw a deep hole in the cliff face, a perfect handhold just beneath the top of the facade. Reaching out, she plunged her arm into it and dragged herself up, bringing her face level with the hole. Looking into it, she saw the hollow went back much further than she thought. It was almost a tunnel into the cliff face. Far within it she saw something, hidden in shadow. As she peered into the hollow, the object in the shadows moved.

Its top half rotated around to face her, and she gasped as a pair of glowing orange eyes opened and glared at her from the gloom. She tried to climb away from the hole but before she could move the shadows exploded and the great ash-grey owl hurtled at her face, shrieking.

Powerful wings slammed against her face, hooked talons raked her scalp. Amiel cried out and beat the creature away with her left hand, trying to keep her grip with her right. Blood dripped into her eyes and the world turned red as her handhold crumbled away in mud and dust.

As Amiel began to fall, droplets of blood and grey feathers around her, regret painted her thoughts. Not at

154

her own death, but because she knew she wouldn't see the end of the mission, what was waiting for them beyond the gates. It was over now. All done.

A powerful hand reached down and caught her arm. The grip tightened, and her fall ended. Looking up, her eyes filled with blood, Amiel could only see a vague outline of her saviour.

"Jenvilno?" the word was out of her mouth before she knew it was in her thoughts. The grip was so strong. Who else could it be but the warrior? Amiel smiled, delirious with fear. He wouldn't let her fall. But when the figure spoke, his voice was deep and warm, and nothing like the few words she had heard the masked fighter speak.

"No, no," he chuckled. "Now, grab my arm and try to find a foothold, and we'll pull you up."

Blinking blood from her eyes, Amiel looked down long enough to set her feet again. She reached up and gripped the wrist of the man on the cliff. Pushing with her feet, she felt other arms grab her as she rose, helping her over the ledge. Her head spinning, terror and elation vying for supremacy in her heart, she could only roll onto her back in the cool, wet grass and lie panting, her eyes closed. When she found the strength to open them again, she saw that the night had cleared during their lengthy climb. The weak moonlight over the ruined town had given way to a clear night sky, full of stars. For as long as she could remember, since she had first marched out on her suicide mission, she had been trapped, smothered under a grey sky and blankets of mist. She saw the stars for the first time and she smiled.

"See? She's fine. Tough, this one. That cut doesn't even need stitching. It's closing already."

The voice of the man who had saved her. Amiel sat up and, though still shaking a little, managed to climb to her feet. Before her, four soldiers stood. Three men and a woman, watching her expectantly. A little beyond them, facing away, Jenvilno waited.

"Are you all right?" one of the soldiers, a big man with a thick beard, spoke to Amiel in the voice she knew. She wiped blood from the owl's wound. The man was right, it was clotting already.

"Yes," she managed to answer. "Thank you for catching me, are you-?"

A friendly smile lit the man's broad face. "From the gate? Yes. We were sent to light the signals for you, but we were only just in time to meet your friend and stop you from falling."

The man meant Jenvilno, but when he spoke of her friend Amiel immediately thought of Axel. She turned in a panic, but relief bloomed in her when she saw him struggling over the edge of the cliff. Amiel turned and looked into the soldier's eyes. His friendly smile remained fixed, but he only held her gaze. After a silent moment, Amiel turned and dashed to the precipice. She supported Axel as he climbed up, and the two leaned on each other as they walked back to the soldiers. The soldier's words occurred to her suddenly.

"The signals?" she asked. "What do you mean?"

"Those over there," the soldier answered. "We wanted to show you the way."

Amiel looked where he was pointing, and saw the stakes jutting from the ground at the cliff edge. Their tops were wrapped with layers of thick cloth, round bundles which looked like misshapen skulls from a distance.

"Are you ready then? The Palace is down that path."

Amiel turned, her mind thrown into confusion.

"Palace?" The Savage lived in a tent sewn from the skin of his enemies. He lived in a tower of bones or a den of snakes. He did not live in a palace.

"Yes. He's waiting for us there. Come now."

The soldiers turned and began to walk along a neat

stone path set into the waving grass. Amiel followed them, the youth and the masked fighter falling into step behind her. The path led down a gentle slope, but before long the hill dropped away sharply, the meadow falling into a deep valley. Amiel saw the river re-emerging from the choking weeds that had forced them through the town and over the cliff. Its waters cleansed now, it sparkled in the starlight, but it was the building the water flowed past that grabbed and held Amiel's gaze. The sprawling palace covered most of the valley floor, its great towers stroking the face of the heavens, shining with the light of a thousand golden flames. Next to her, the soldier who had saved her spoke with pride.

"Welcome to the gate of Belenos."

Mythmaking: Part Four

Janvier will come now to the gate of the Savage. The Savage is evil and cruel. He thirsts for blood, and his wall is covered with the skulls of his enemies. He will demand to hear tales of Janvier's strength. The knight will tell him that he is Janvier who wields mighty Lux, who is friend to giants and who outwitted the Great Trickster. He will say he is Janvier who prayed with the Priest, and laid him to rest. He is Janvier, and no man is mightier.

But the Savage will only laugh a devil's laugh at the noble knight's words. He will gnash his pointed teeth and promise that at the end of their fight, Janvier's skull will be next to hang on his wall.

The next day will dawn, Janvier and the Savage will begin their fight. The Savage's evil is great, as is his power and speed. He wields a great sword of sharpened bone, and Janvier will know his most dangerous fight is upon him. For hours they will fight, and though both will deal terrible injuries to their opponent, neither will best the other. Mighty Lux will spill the blood of the Savage, and the vicious bone-sword will pierce the armour of virtuous Janvier, tearing deep into the flesh within. Janvier will know that if they keep fighting this way, both will die, and he will never reach Deseme. He will throw down his sword and offer friendship to the Savage, even as the monster raises his bone-sword to slaughter the noble knight.

The Savage will be impressed by Janvier's bravery, for the knight will look into his terrifying enemy's eyes with no fear. The Savage too will drop his sword of sharpened bone, and take Janvier's hands in his.

And so, the noble knight will walk on, triumphant not through blood and combat, but through mercy and peace.

Chapter Twenty-Nine

Where the other gates had been locked, the gate of Belenos stood open.

Huge columns lined the entrance to the palace, holding up a great roof of pale stone. The front of this pediment was carved intricately, the stone cut into a scene depicting the heavens and, at the centre, a vast sun. Amiel looked from this to the mighty towers rising behind it, lit by beacons burning the night away. Why did the Savage live in such a place? Had he murdered the rightful owner and occupied it? As they moved beyond the entrance, they came into a wide courtyard bordered by marble slabs. Neat grass covered the ground within this perimeter, and at the centre stood a fountain. Amiel paused to study it. Again, it showed the heavens. Stars and planets circled up around a central column of cloud, and at the top, dwarfing the others, was the orb of the sun. Water flowed from the top of the sun, cascading downward and spiralling over the other carvings to splash into the pool at the bottom. Across the surface of the sun, one word was inscribed. *Invictus.* Unconquered. The word came from an ancient language of the Empire, a different one to that spoken by the Priest as he damned Jenvilno. It was unfathomable why it would be carved here, so far beyond the boundaries of civilisation.

Droplets flew from the water's surface, shining in the light of more torches. The soldier who led them paused too, and one hand drifted out to stroke the central pillar of cloud and stars. The touch was reverent, and water flowed over his gentle fingers. For another moment he was silent, staring at the sun. The soldier looked away, beyond the fountain which still splashed quietly in the night.

"Come now."

He led the way again. Amiel was about to follow when Axel caught her sleeve.

"Amiel," he said. She knew immediately what he was talking about.

All around them, the courtyard was encircled by a colonnade. From its many arches, emerging from the shadows into the light of the flames, came scores of people. Men and women, tall and beautiful, their faces patrician. They wore fine clothes, and carried themselves like lords and kings. Amiel's hand strayed to her sword, but these newcomers showed no hostility. They talked to one another, chuckled and joked, and their glances at the three travellers held no malice. Soft footsteps rustled on the grass next to Amiel as Jenvilno moved after the soldier. She turned and walked after the masked warrior, flanked by Axel. Behind them, the men and women in the expensive clothes followed at a distance, but their soft conversation did not hush and Amiel felt no threat from them. She tried to listen to them, tried to hear individual words, but their voices were muffled somehow, indistinct.

With their new entourage, Amiel and the others walked through the open courtyard into the body of the palace. All around them was smooth, polished stone, gleaming even in the sparse light. No tapestries hung on the wall, no statues stood in honour of the lord. Again, Amiel thought of the Savage awaiting them. Had he torn down the tapestries? Smashed the statues to erase the memory of the man he had usurped in this great hall? She glanced back at the expensive dress of those who followed them. They could be prisoners of the Savage. But their easy manner made this seem unlikely. Were they his allies, their appearance hiding their true nature? Amiel thought of sneering Lord Gwydion and his surprising skill, and the emaciated Priest's insanity-born power, and reminded herself that appearances could deceive. Events were unfolding in order, but the details were twisted into darker shapes.

Two sets of footsteps echoed on floors of polished marble. Jenvilno's feet made no sound as they worked their way toward the heart of the palace. Ahead of them, their guide led them seemingly at random down one gleaming corridor after another. Behind them, the crowd of nobles followed. Amiel didn't know how long they walked in that palace, lost in the endless white. Only the presence of Axel next to her calmed her as she followed a route she didn't understand. Finally, the man stopped by a great arch cut into a wall of smooth stone.

"Step inside. The lord will be here soon." His earlier smiles were only a memory, his face now remained set in solemnity. Amiel led the other two through the arch, into a room that made her gasp with its beauty.

Simple, largely unadorned, the throne room of Lord Belenos was vast. Its ceilings were high, and its walls were lined with huge arched windows, letting in both the silver moonlight and the torch flames burning around the palace exterior. Polished stone shone around them, and a simple carpet woven from a fabric of dark purple led them toward the towering throne at the back, carved from the same smooth stone as the room itself and sparingly decorated with pale gold. They followed the carpet, approaching the throne. The men and women following began to fill the room behind them, spreading out into a crowd. Their conversation gradually grew louder as their number grew. Axel murmured something to Amiel, but she couldn't hear his words over their noise.

Lost in thought, she stared at the throne. They were moments away from seeing the Savage. Questions again assailed her. Why did he choose to live in this palace? If he had murdered its rightful owner, why was it perfect, and why had he not sullied the walls with blood? Where were the skulls of his enemies? Would the three of them be the first in his collection? Amiel's hand strayed to her sword, and this time she let it rest there. The Savage was barely more than an animal. He may attack without a word. She steeled herself for what she might see as the soldier appeared, walking to the side of the throne and raising a hand. Immediately the crowd fell into silence. He spoke only two words.

"Lord Belenos."

Amiel waited, tense, but nothing happened. After endless seconds of silence, only the shuffling of the shifting crowd behind them broke the stillness. Amiel's heart felt swollen in her chest. She looked around. She couldn't see any place from which the Savage might emerge. There must be a hidden door.

Then it came to her too late. The sound of human movement. The crowd parting behind them. Letting someone through. She whirled, her hand grasping for her sword. She was too slow. He was through the crowd and walking toward them. Amiel's hand fell away from her sword, her eyes grew wide at what she saw.

Chapter Thirty

The man who strode toward them was tall, taller even than Jenvilno. His shoulders were massive, broad and thick with muscle. His arms hung at his sides, huge strength coiled through his sinews. His body was covered with a simple short robe, hanging to his knees. He walked with power and purpose, long steps closing the distance between him and the travellers quickly. Amiel's hand left her sword and fell to her side.

His skin was dark, but not as dark as her own. His black hair seemed to curl slightly like hers, too. But with his short, military cut, it was hard for her to tell. His shaved temples were turning to silver, though he had the body of a man in his prime. His face was strong, but his features had a delicacy and kindness about them, a nobility. His eyes were a deep, intriguing gold in colour, and full of warmth as he smiled at the three newcomers. He stepped past them, climbed the two steps to his throne, and sat. He rested one elbow on his knee, covered by the white and gold robe, and favoured them again with his smile.

"Warriors," he said in a rich voice from deep within his massive chest. "You have reached my gate. Congratulations, and welcome."

Amiel stepped forward, shock, relief and confusion vying for supremacy in her soul. Next to her, Axel approached the throne too, taking off his hat and holding it to his chest. Belenos spoke again.

"No challenger has ever come this far. The Priest has great strength, and his faith drives him to fight with a fury most cannot hope to overcome."

"He had great strength," Amiel admitted. "But he did not survive the fight. He lies in his church now, and forever."

Belenos inclined his head slowly, his face serious. "You laid him to rest? His crusade is over? I am glad. There were too many bodies in that forest. Too many lost souls, though a few escaped. I can only hope his belief remained to comfort him in his final moments, and he at last realised he sacrificed so many and prayed so fervently to a false god."

His words were spoken from his heart, and in his face was pain. Amiel felt strange, seeing this honour from a man who barred their path.

"Why?" Amiel asked suddenly. "Why does someone as noble as you fight for him?"

"For whom?" Belenos asked, his golden eyes resting on Amiel.

She had to struggle to force the words out, to sully the air with his name.

"For Decius." Her voice echoed in the hollow of the great room, set the crowd behind them to murmuring. "You are his ally, are you not? You killed all those people in the town, didn't you?"

Belenos shook his head, "Me? An ally of that... of Decius?" he asked. "No, I am not his ally. Nor was it I who killed those innocent people, though I did bury them with respect. He ventured beyond his citadel and murdered them. Long before I took over this gate. His thirst for blood is terrible, and no one is safe from him, when he rides out."

He sat back in his throne now, his forearms resting on the armrests, his back straight. His face was grave when he spoke again. "I am an enemy of Decius, and always will be."

"But it is your place to guard this gate," Amiel countered. "It is your purpose to keep us out. We who would kill Decius. How can you do that, and claim to be his enemy?"

"It is my place to keep out all but the strongest," Belenos answered. "For they are the only ones with any hope. Only those who can defeat me may continue onward. Only those who prove stronger can pass by, first to the final gate and then beyond, to look upon Decius himself."

"You said the Priest prayed to a false god." Words rushed from Amiel now, as if drawn through her from elsewhere. "Is Decius not a god? Does he not await us in his cathedral? At every gate we hear a new story. I am tired of it. I ask you now. Who is Decius?"

Belenos did not answer at first. When he spoke at last, his voice was soft, his words heavy with sadness.

"And I tell you this, soldier. Anyone who seeks an answer to that question, beyond simply 'he is Decius', will find only misery."

Amiel tried to speak, but she could find no more words. The strange moment passed, and Belenos smiled his warm smile once more, leaning forward in his throne again, speaking to them but raising his voice for the benefit of the crowd.

"Are any of you strong enough to pass to the next gate? I hope so. Make yourself known, you who would challenge me."

Amiel and Axel looked now to Jenvilno. The masked fighter stood still. Amiel saw his grey eyes, staring from behind the metal at the lord in white and gold. She looked from one to the other. The masked man's dark clothes hung from his wiry frame. Once so fine, his jacket was torn and dirtied now from the journey through the forest, bloodied from fighting and killing. Godlike Belenos reflected him, his perfect opposite. The lord's clothing was flawless, his body honed. She didn't know who would win. But if Belenos was hiding a savage nature behind his exterior and a horrible fate awaited those challengers who lost, she could only hope and trust in the great strength of the mysterious fighter. Of the saint. Of Janvier.

Belenos saw where the other two were looking. He

smiled at the mask, never faltering even under the cold gaze of the grey eyes.

"You are my opponent?" He looked at the great crowd gathered in the room, then back to the man before him. "Good. Step forward, then. State your name and deeds."

Slowly, the masked man walked toward the throne. Amiel nodded to herself. He stopped before the lord, and the crowd strained to hear his words.

"I am Jenvilno."

Belenos waited in silence, but no more words came from behind the mask.

"It is late," finally he spoke to the group. "And you must be tired from your journey. My men will prepare your rooms. I hope you like them. Explore the palace until then, and they will collect you when your accommodation is ready. We fight tomorrow, Jenvilno. Prepare yourself."

Belenos sat back, raised his hand in a gesture. From the crowd behind them, three soldiers walked forward. One gestured for Amiel to follow him. With exhaustion finally catching up to her, she followed, grateful. The crowd parted to let her through.

Chapter Thirty-One

She found Axel in the courtyard with the fountain. He was sitting alone on a stone bench, and on all sides the fine-clothed courtiers of Belenos surrounded him. They sat on other benches or stood at the fountain's edge, on the neat grass and marble floors, where their chatter merged with the whisper of the water. They turned as one to look at Amiel as she came in. None of them looked at Axel, but she assumed he had received the same treatment when he entered the courtyard ahead of her.

She barely gave them a glance, taking in only their strange, archaic dress and blurred glimpses of faces as they turned away from her. She walked over to the boy where he sat, and joined him on the bench.

"This isn't what I was expecting," she told him.

"Me neither," he admitted. "Beyond the very basic framework you described, everything seems to be unfolding very differently. Maybe you were right. Maybe you all heard the idealised version of the story, and this is the way it has to happen in the real world, whatever "it" is."

"What do you mean?" Amiel asked.

"Well, the story you have told is of the saint who sails to kill the Mad King," Axel said. "But you are describing figures and events from long ago, or which haven't happened yet. I know something strange is happening, and I know it is vaguely unfolding parallel to your story. But I am still not convinced he is a saint, and that *Theos* sent him on this mission. I am not even sure *Theos* exists. I think maybe the stories and myths were built up over time, and what we are seeing is the nasty reality. And that... scares me."

"Why does it scare you? As you say, the major events will remain the same."

"Will they? They have so far, but with each gate we deviate more and more. We went from the Giant to the Trickster who I fought and... killed. From there, we got the frenzied zealot where you expected a benevolent priest. Now we have a kind and virtuous aristocrat where I was expecting a cannibalistic maniac. Your saint is getting darker, angrier and more violent as we pass each gate. We're spiralling further and further away from what you expect. How do you know we won't break away from whatever story the Janvier myth is based on as we travel further up? How do you know we can even succeed?"

"I... I don't," Amiel admitted. "All I have is my faith. But we have to go on. We have to finish this. I am more certain than ever that the evil of Decius must be eradicated. We have heard confused and contradicting stories about him, but what Belenos said couldn't have been clearer. He is a monster. Whatever he is, he must be killed. You saw what he did in that town."

"And your hometown," Axel said, nodding.

Amiel started. She kept her face still, not wanting Axel to know how little she had thought of Holheim since they passed the first gate. She had almost forgotten the besieged town entirely. Her previous mission, her punishment, seemed like a comforting dream she had shaken off when she stepped into the trees, awake.

"Yes. He and his men must answer for much," she told him. "Once Jenvilno and Belenos have... once it is over, there is only one final gate before we reach him."

"I still cannot reconcile Belenos with your myth," Axel said. "He seems so noble. Though of course he could be hiding his savage nature until the fight tomorrow."

Amiel recoiled from his careless words, thinking of the general's followers, gathered all around them.

"Axel!" she hissed. "Be quiet! Any of them could

hear us and tell him."

Axel looked at her strangely.

"What are you talking about?"

She didn't look around, not wanting to alert the nobles.

"If one of them goes to him with what you just said, none of us will be safe."

Axel looked around, his confusion turning to worry as his eyes returned to her.

"Amiel, there's no one else here."

"What? Don't be ridiculous. They're-" Amiel finally looked away from Axel, and faltered. The courtyard was empty, the murmur of voices was merely the sound of the gentle fountain. Her stomach twisted. They must have left while she and Axel were talking. Only... why hadn't she heard anything? Why hadn't they so much as glanced at him?

"They were here," she insisted. "They..." she stood and scanned the empty courtyard. There was no suggestion they had ever been here. A soft noise drew her wild eyes, but it was only a pair of the general's soldiers, entering through a colonnade to her right.

"Your rooms are ready," the one on the left addressed her. "I suggest you sleep and prepare for the trial tomorrow."

Without turning to Axel, she marched after the soldier who had spoken to her. She almost stumbled, and pretended she didn't hear the boy stutter her name as she left.

Chapter Thirty-Two

Amiel couldn't sleep. Lying back on fine bedclothes of rich purple, fully clothed, she stared at the high ceiling of her room, waiting. Her guide had taken her up seven flights of stairs, led her into this magnificent room, and then left her alone. Alone to think. And so, now she tried to sleep, and now her thoughts kept her awake. The eerie moment in the courtyard had been only the latest of far too many troubling events she had faced. She longed to be outside once again, but she feared she would lose herself in the dark palace if she tried to find a way out. Sighing, she rolled from the bed and stood up. Over against the far wall she saw a curtain, the same purple as her bedclothes. It covered the entire wall, and she wondered what was behind it. Grasping one edge, she pulled it to one side, and almost smiled.

The heavy curtain obscured a doorway leading out onto a balcony. Stepping out, Amiel breathed deep, feeling the constriction of the room falling away from her slender shoulders. She walked to the wall running along the edge of the stone balcony and looked out over the valley. With mild surprise, she saw that she was on the side opposite to the way they had entered the palace. She could see where next they would travel if Jenvilno was victorious. Beyond the walls of the palace, the river continued along the flat floor of the valley, beneath a clear sky burning with stars. Its waters were calm and peaceful, still glittering with whatever minerals it picked up in the rockface they had climbed. Amiel's breath came slow, and in her heart, she tried to find the same stillness which blanketed the valley.

"Good evening."

When the voice came from her left, she didn't start. She only looked to its source. Belenos stood next to her, leaning on the balcony wall to her left. He moved silently, delicately for such a big man, and Amiel felt her fears for the coming fight return. She looked past Belenos, and saw that the balcony extended further than the wall of her room alone. It stretched along the entire side of the palace, faced by many other doors. One of them must be the room of Belenos, she reasoned.

"You can't sleep, can you?" he asked, not discouraged by her lack of a response. "I saw in the throne room. There is confusion in you, and fear. But strength also, and faith."

He smiled as he said this last word. His eyes seemed sad, the gold of his irises subdued in the darkness. Towering over her, he placed a huge, gentle hand on her shoulder.

"Your mission is a gruelling one, your journey arduous. You are strong, but your soul carries a burden alone. So just for me, soldier, not for a crowd. State your name and deeds."

Amiel opened her mouth to refuse politely.

"Everything is going wrong," she told Belenos. "I thought I was in a myth, a story from my youth. I thought it was becoming a prophecy, coming true. The knight Janvier would sail up the river to find the Mad King Deseme. He would fight his way through the gates, defeating the Generals. The Giant, the Trickster, the Priest. They all appeared. But they weren't quite right. None of it happened correctly. Here we were supposed to find the Savage, and instead we find you, Belenos. You're noble and kind... you're no beast. How will the noble knight tame you if you're not the Savage? I don't know if the myth is coming true in a twisted way... or not coming true at all. I don't know if what I've seen is just coincidence, or what I've been waiting for. But most of all, I don't-"

She faltered briefly. She looked down at the floor. When she looked again at the face of Belenos, her eyes were full of tears.

"I don't know why I need to believe this so *much,*" she admitted. "When Axel doubted me, when he didn't believe too, it made me so angry. And I don't know why. Even now, I almost want you to be cruel, to be a monster beneath all the kindness. Because then it would be *right.*"

Words failed her again. She dropped her eyes. This time, she could not raise her head to look at Belenos when she spoke.

"He scares me, too."

She paused, took a deep breath.

"*Him.*" she said. "He's meant to be Janvier. *He's* the one meant to be noble. But sometimes I look into those eyes behind the mask and I see such rage. Like when he killed the Priest. Jenvilno butchered him, cut him down. Janvier would never do that. Don't you see? Never. Sometimes I look at him, and all I see is a murderer and a monster. But still I need... still I need to believe he's Janvier! What's..."

As her voice dropped to a whisper, she finally met the lord's eyes for the last time.

"What's happening to me?"

Belenos said nothing. Amiel heard only the sound of the river far below. He stared into her eyes, no expression on his face. He dropped his hand from her shoulder, turned away.

"I need to prepare for tomorrow." His voice had no tone. It was as if she hadn't spoken. He walked away. "Goodbye."

Chapter Thirty-Three

The day of their fight dawned bright and clear, but cold. Awake and dressed long before the sun came up, Amiel watched the light crawl through the valley. Shreds of mist shone at first as the golden light struck them, then vanished into nothingness under its glare. She wished the sun could burn away the lingering dreams that had plagued her brief sleep.

"It's time."

Amiel slowly turned to see one of Belenos' soldiers. The man waited for her curt nod, then turned and walked from the balcony. She followed him through her room and into the endless corridors. He led her up further still. Together they climbed flight after flight of steps. As they ascended, the air grew colder and the light of the sun grew brighter. His silence gave Amiel time to think, and her thoughts kept returning to the previous night's strange conversation with Belenos. Why had he asked her to speak, only to ignore her? Amiel had hoped her doubts, her confusion and her fear would drain away when she voiced them, but Belenos' inexplicable reaction had only made them worse. She banished them as best she could. What would happen would happen, she tried to tell herself. All that mattered was their mission, and the next gate. But still her stomach felt twisted and tight, and still she replayed Belenos' few words in her mind as they climbed the final flight of stairs and emerged into the freezing outer air.

They were on the roof of the main palace building itself. At its four corners, the mightiest towers thrust upward to the heavens, the spaces between them interspersed with smaller turrets. But even where they stood, Amiel knew the view of the valley below would be spectacular. She knew she would see all the way to the next gate, to the House of Decius itself. But her view was blocked by the tiers of seats that formed an obscuring wall around the flat rooftop.

The expanse of roof they stood on, she realised, formed the great floor of an ancient eastern-style amphitheatre, surrounded by rising seats. Not one was empty. There were hundreds of stone benches around the area and no excess space to be found. On every side of her she saw crowds of the handsome courtiers who had followed them the previous night. The ones she had seen in the courtyard with Axel, before their mysterious disappearance. There were more than she would have believed possible. They laughed and joked with one another, their murmuring voices like constant bird-chatter. Still she could not hear their words. They looked down at Amiel and the man who had led her there. Amiel froze, daunted by the eyes of so many upon her. She looked in vain for a space in the crowd to lose herself in and when she looked back, her guide had melted away. Discomfort threatened to turn to fear as she felt the gaze of the great mass upon her, like a weight. When a familiar voice reached her, clear over the formless noise of the others, she immediately looked to its source and the corners of her mouth twitched. To her left, Axel sat in the front row, a space next to him. Moving quickly, Amiel vaulted over the low stone wall in front of the first row of seats and took her place next to him. She looked over her shoulder at the people in the crowd, but the sun shone too brightly and she could not discern individual faces in its glaring light. She was about to speak, when the chatter of the crowd became an indistinct, distant roar. Belenos had arrived.

Clad in armour of burning gold, a mighty sun on his chest and his head protected by a bright helm, the kind lord smiled at the crowd. He walked away from the roof staircase, his head raised and his strange eyes shining on either side of the helm's nose-guard. At his waist a huge sword waited, sheathed. Sunlight flashed from his armour as Belenos walked slowly toward the barrier ahead of the front row of seats. His eyes passed over Amiel and his smile didn't flicker, but he didn't acknowledge her. He turned now, his back against the stone barrier. Belenos stood tall, arms folded and massive shoulders squared.

And he waited.

The sound of the crowd seemed to grow further and further away, until at last there was silence. The cold air had a tension in it, and Amiel could feel the anticipation of those around her as keenly as she felt her own. Next to her, Axel barely drew breath.

They waited.

Footsteps cut through the silence. A soft gasp slithered from the throats of the audience, and then all was still again. One after another, slowly, the sound of the steps climbing the stairs echoed impossibly loud in the silence of the massed throng. At the top of the staircase, just beneath the floor of the roof, a shadow formed. A shadow with eyes.

Jenvilno climbed the last few steps, emerging into the sun. Amiel heard sparse whispers around her, rumours slipping from lip to ear, as the masked man set foot on the roof. He paused, his grey eyes sweeping the massive crowd who watched him. The sun flashed on the metal of his mask as his head moved. When his gaze passed over her, Amiel shuddered whereas, before, the cold had not touched her. Jenvilno wore tattered black and grey, contrasting with Belenos' gold. Simple cloth where the lord was armoured. At Jenvilno's waist was his sword, his *Lux*. Amiel looked from this blade to the much greater sword of Belenos, and not for the first time she felt fear for the outcome of the fight.

Belenos raised a hand, and a soldier rushed to his side. The murmuring of the crowd began again as the lord spoke, and the soldier dashed away back down the stairs. Moments later, he returned, with a new weapon for Belenos. A short sword with an ornate handguard. Belenos smiled at the soldier. He reached to take the blade, then drew his hand back. The lord clapped his armoured hands together with two metallic crashes, and two more soldiers were at his side. He spoke to them briefly, then reached for the clasps of his armour. His men stood by as he removed the golden plates from his body. First, he removed the heavy breastplate with its sun emblem, handing it to the first man. Next, he unfastened the greaves from his legs, letting them clatter to the floor. He removed his shining armguards and gauntlets, and the thick belt with its hanging metal links to protect his groin. All of these Belenos left on the floor of the arena. Finally, the lord reached up and took the white-plumed helm from his head. Belenos stood before the silent Jenvilno, stripped of his armour.

His two men gathered up the pieces and took them away. Beneath the metal, he wore his simple white and gold tunic of the night before. Applause rippled softly around the crowd as he now took his new sword from the man who had brought it, and waved him away. Belenos drew his sword and, raising it high, saluted his opponent. Jenvilno stood poised, his legs bent slightly and held apart. His grey eyes were empty, unblinking, as he looked at Belenos. His hand snaked to the hilt of his sword and eased it from its sheath. His grip tightened on it, the frosty light of the sun giving it an ethereal glow. The wind rose, and Belenos raised his massive arms, his voice ringing out clear and true over the crowd.

"Before me stands a new challenger!" he called. "He fights for passage through my gate. If I win, his quest is at an end, and a long journey home awaits him. If he wins, even if I do not survive, you are to let him through. You are to send him on his way down the river, with your blessings. He will be treated with the honour of a true victor."

As the echoes of his shout died away, Lord Belenos turned to the masked man. The lord was close to Amiel's seat and she heard his next words, though he spoke them to Jenvilno alone.

"May you fight well, swordsman."

They began.

Chapter Thirty-Four

Jenvilno moved first. His shadow, made elongated and grotesque by the cold sun above, stretched out from beneath his feet. Its blackness on the stone ground engulfed Lord Belenos as the masked fighter sprinted toward him. Amiel saw Belenos smile, saw his hand tighten around the hilt of his sword. The audience cheered as they clashed.

Jenvilno's arm drew back. His blade flashed out in a murderous slash toward the lord's neck. With one deft movement, Belenos raised his own sword and blocked the blow. The masked fighter attacked twice more, but each time the lord parried the blows. Now the golden-eyed lord attacked, and it was Jenvilno defending. Belenos was huge, but his speed was incredible. He fought with a skill and finesse Amiel had never seen before. She thought of the Priest, his power fuelled by faith and rage. He had been fast and strong, but he had known nothing about true skill, and he had died for it. She watched Jenvilno, pushed back by the calm, precise assault of Belenos, and she knew she had been right to be wary of the golden lord.

Jenvilno stepped around the blade of Belenos and hurled himself at his opponent once more. Belenos evaded the strike and raised his own blade. Amiel cringed as the lord's attack came with terrible speed. Jenvilno raised his sword to block, but the massive lord smashed it to one side. Jenvilno barely kept his grip on the blade, and he stumbled. Amiel's heart thundered as she saw the masked warrior vulnerable to at least three different killing strikes from Belenos. She thought of the power Belenos fought with, and his strange, cold treatment of her the night before. She knew then that the Savage was rising within him, and Jenvilno was about to die.

Belenos followed up his attack, his blade aimed at Jenvilno's sword-hand, a disarming blow. Jenvilno recovered fast, spun around the attack. When he struck back, he aimed for the lord's eyes. Belenos raised his blade before his face, and caught the strike of the masked warrior. Their swords clashed together inches from his flesh, but the lord did not flinch or blink. Jenvilno pressed his attack, trying to force his sword point forward, but the strength of his opponent held the blade at bay. The audience applauded the combatants.

Belenos looked into Jenvilno's eyes, and whatever he saw there made him raise one eyebrow, his face calm.

"To the death then, swordsman?" Amiel heard him say. "As you wish."

Belenos thrust his sword forward, against Jenvilno's blade, pushing the masked man away from him. Jenvilno stumbled backward into a half crouch. The sun flashed from his mask still, but as he turned his head, Amiel glimpsed his eyes behind the mask and felt her terror grow. She saw the strange light blazing in them once more. She remembered the priest, cut down as he spat defiance. She remembered the silent rage of Jenvilno. For an inexplicable second, she remembered the Hall of Jotun, Jenvilno's eyes shining in the torchlight as he left the room. The memories vanished from her thoughts as the fighter crouched lower, then threw himself at Belenos.

The lord blocked three more blows, then sent back a cut of his own. Amiel's heart leapt as his blade opened a small cut on Jenvilno's upper arm. She almost smiled before she realised what she was doing. They needed to defeat Belenos to get through the gate. Why was she almost cheering for him? Why did she feel fear when she saw the rage in the eyes of Jenvilno? Rage he needed, to win against a mighty adversary? She looked at Axel, but he was lost in the fight. She returned her gaze to the fighters.

Jenvilno attacked again, and again. Savage cuts, trying to impale or disembowel the great lord. But he could not break through the iron guard of Belenos. The huge man was unbeatable. He slammed down blow after blow and Jenvilno could barely keep himself safe. With every attack turned aside, and every scratch the lord inflicted on his flesh, Amiel saw Jenvilno growing angrier. His eyes shone with their grey fire as he grew reckless. He attacked with more ferocity, but none of the grace Amiel had seen in all of his fights until now. Belenos' sword raked Jenvilno's shoulder, injured in the fight with the Priest, but the wound was not serious. The lord sliced a shallow cut in the skin above Jenvilno's knee, but again it was not severe. Jenvilno's attacks grew in savagery and power, his blows would have shattered the bones of lesser men, torn their flesh and left them dying. But Belenos was no lesser man. He was the superior swordsman, and Jenvilno was losing.

The masked fighter struck again, his breath coming harsh and ragged from behind the metal mask now, each exhale almost a snarl. His black clothes were torn, stained with fresh blood and the dried filth of the forest. Before him Belenos stood perfect and unmarked in his fine tunic, still gleaming white. Amiel knew Jenvilno's rage. She had felt it herself against opponents she thought she couldn't beat. But it was vital to control that rage. To use it, but to fight without anger or passion. She looked at Jenvilno and knew he had lost himself, knew he was ruled by his fury.

She knew he was already defeated.

Jenvilno's blade scythed out, his speed frightening. But Belenos was faster. The lord blocked two fast blows from the right, and a thrust to his heart. His own blade shone as he raised it high, and brought it slashing downward toward Jenvilno's throat. The masked warrior threw himself backward, but not fast enough. The razor tip of Belenos' sword slid through the sleeve of Jenvilno's jacket, cutting into his forearm. A hiss of breath behind the mask, and Amiel knew their champion was in great pain. Jenvilno backed away, blood already beginning to seep from his shredded sleeve. He looked down at the wound, then angrily raised his sword to his shoulder. Amiel was mystified until Jenvilno began cutting away the sleeves from his jacket. First, he took away the ruined one, throwing it to the floor. Next, he cut away the intact one from his uninjured arm. It joined the other on the floor, and Amiel now looked upon the masked warrior's bare arms. They were slender but powerful, sinewy muscles standing out beneath the skin. The injury on his forearm still bled, but he ignored it. He stepped forward again.

Belenos held up a hand. "You wish to fight on, with such an injury? Swordsman, you are good, but I am better. I am Belenos, I am unconquered. You cannot defeat me. Stand down now, and live."

For a frozen second, Jenvilno stared at the man before him. Without warning, he charged, his blade held loose at his side, low, ready to gut golden Belenos. The crowd was silent, anticipating another great clash.

Then the noise began.

Amiel looked around, confused. Over the sound of the crowd it was impossible to tell where the haunting howl was coming from. She felt cold, and her lips moved in a silent prayer when she realised the inhuman sound was coming from behind the mask. It was a scream of rage. Jenvilno's eyes smouldered with their frenzied light. Around Amiel and Axel, the crowd gasped in fear.

Belenos was ready for him. The golden lord blocked the masked man's attacks. He stepped around one blow, still so agile for a man of his size. He hammered another blow to Jenvilno's injured forearm with the handguard of his sword. Jenvilno staggered, and Belenos moved in to end the fight. He brought his sword down in a brutal blow on Jenvilno's own blade. The masked fighter fell to one knee, and lost his grip on the sword. Amiel cried out as *Lux* spun from his grasp. The sword clattered to the stone, the light from the sun striking it and glinting from its blade. It came to rest at the feet of Belenos.

With a smile, the lord reached down and took Jenvilno's blade, holding his own in the other hand.

"Swordsman, you fought well," he bowed his head in respect. "Against anyone else you would have been triumphant."

A few long strides took Belenos to the centre of the arena. His back to his defeated enemy, who still crouched on one knee. The lord raised his arms, ready to address the crowd. Around them, the throng began to cheer. Amiel was numb. It was over. They were defeated. Over the roar of the crowd, she spoke.

"Axel... what... what happened?" Her voice sounded strange, distant to her own ears.

"Don't you realise, Amiel? You were right, it's happening." Axel's voice was flat like hers, all emotion shocked from it. "The noble knight won."

Belenos stood arms raised, waiting for the crowd to grow quiet. Beautiful he stood, triumphant, unconquered still, the sunlight shining from him. He was still waiting when Jenvilno spoke. Four soft words plunged the crowd into silence, and terrified Amiel.

"You think you've won?"

Chapter Thirty-Five

A hush descended on the arena. All eyes turned to the masked man. He still crouched on one knee, one fist braced against the arena floor. His eyes never left Belenos. But as those four words left his hidden lips, he began to rise. Amiel's terror approached panic as she saw his eyes behind the mask. There was nothing in them, none of the rage which had burned there moments ago. His voice was flat, toneless. But her heart threatened to stop and she trembled uncontrollably as he climbed to his feet. He no longer stood straight, but in a half-hunched, predatory posture, his spine twisted. His fists clenched before him, Jenvilno began to stalk toward Belenos.

"You think you've won?"

There was no emotion in the sound, nothing recognisably human. Amiel thought of creatures she had heard about that could mimic words, with no understanding of their meaning. The crowd watched Jenvilno, making no sound. Amiel looked at the masses around her in disbelief. How could they not see? How did they not know the danger their lord was in? She turned her eyes to Belenos himself. He watched the masked man too, a kind smile shining on his defeated opponent as the distance between them closed.

"Swordsman, it is over." Belenos spoke in a warm voice. In his hands he held his own sword and Jenvilno's, but he reached out in a gesture of peace, of reconciliation. Too late, Amiel's voice slashed through the dead air.

"Belenos, *no!*" she screamed. But the lord was already approaching his fallen opponent, arms open.

Jenvilno's hand shot out, snapped shut around the golden lord's neck. Belenos choked as the terrible grip grew tight, and from numb hands the two swords fell. The lord's hands gripped Jenvilno's arm, and though Amiel saw the huge muscles straining, saw the knuckles turning pale, Belenos could not break the hold on his throat.

Slowly, so slowly, Jenvilno dragged Belenos forward, downward, until his face was almost touching the metal of the mask. Still his voice was hollow, still it slid quietly, softly, from his throat.

"Disarming me *is... not... enough.*"

The storm began.

Jenvilno's other hand, loose at his side, began to twitch. Suddenly, it clenched into a fist. Jenvilno pulled back, and hammered a blow into Belenos' face. The crowd gasped, and Amiel heard scattered screams as the lord stumbled. He tried to right himself, but Jenvilno's fist rose and fell, rose and fell again. It cracked against Belenos' face, tore skin and slammed down onto bone. Again, and again Jenvilno drew back and struck, and Belenos could only struggle worthlessly. He raised one hand to guard his face, but Jenvilno forced it aside with his forearm and struck again. Belenos shone in gold and crimson now, blood flowing from his mangled lips and cut face, bright on his dark skin. He coughed around Jenvilno's choking hand and threw his arms forward. An attempt to make peace, or perhaps a feeble attack. Jenvilno ignored Belenos' hands. His fist thundered down again, another devastating blow. Another. Jenvilno attacked faster now, his arm spattered to the elbow with blood. From his own wound or from his victim, Amiel didn't know. He drove his knuckles backhand into the lord's jaw three times, four. The lord almost fell, but Jenvilno's ruthless grip held him upright, locked in place.

But as Jenvilno's hand grew slick with his blood, Belenos managed to slip away from the stranglehold on his neck. He fell away and half-turned, his faltering flight taking him toward the stone barrier where Amiel and

Axel sat. Before his hands clapped to his face, Amiel saw something red, something mangled. Behind him, Jenvilno stalked forward with jerking steps, his eyes staring at the lord, still blank. There was no uncontrolled aggression in his fighting now, only precision. He laid a hand on Belenos' shoulder and spun the lord back to face him. He hit Belenos again from the right. From the left. Twice again from the right. His whole weight, his expert technique, all of his horrifying power, lay behind every strike. Belenos staggered backward with each blow, blinded by blood, arms held up in useless defence. His legs collapsed again and he dropped to one knee before Jenvilno. The masked man scythed an elbow downward, and Amiel's cry joined the voices of the crowd as the blow crunched through the kneeling man's collarbone. If Belenos screamed, it was lost beneath the noise. Jenvilno drew his arm back and struck the broken bone with his fist, amid shouts rising from the crowd. Two more blows to Belenos' face, three to the broken collarbone, then again Jenvilno's hand locked around the other man's throat and hauled him to his feet once more. Three times the lord tried to escape again, but each time Jenvilno's grasping hand caught on something, his wrist or a fold of tunic, and dragged him back into the onslaught. Belenos was too weak to fight back, too slow to save his eye. Blood stained his close-cropped hair and spread in huge patches on his tunic.

Amiel wanted to move, to run away, but she was frozen as the two fighters finally reached the stone barrier in front of her. Jenvilno pinned the lord back against the smooth stone. Cornered, the lord had no way to escape. His shoulder was a mess of broken bone, drenched in blood. His other arm spasmed, but he couldn't raise it in any sort of defence.

Jenvilno never slowed his assault. He made no sound, but the crack of fist against bone echoed over the crowd. Left, right. Left, right. A brutal march. Relentless, he savaged the trapped Belenos.

Amiel stood, her legs moving without her command. She meant to step forward, to help the lord somehow. To drag him away from the animal in the mask. A hand stopped her. She whipped around and snarled at Axel.

"Let me go!" she ordered. "I have to-"

"*He'll kill you too!*" Axel's shout drove the fury from Amiel with the force of a blow. His next words were smaller, almost broken. "If you go near him, he'll kill you too."

Her strength slid from her body, and Amiel sank back into her seat. Against her will, her eyes turned back to the execution.

Jenvilno's fist drew back again, and he slammed three final blows into the face of his enemy. Belenos sagged over. Grotesque, his head bent backward and backward, reaching an unnatural angle, almost wrapping around the stone lip of the barrier. Upside-down, his ruined face regarded Amiel. His beauty was gone now, buried beneath blood and torn flesh. His one functioning eye was dull, stripped of its powerful light, its deep gold faded. Even as a seasoned soldier of a dozen dirty wars, Amiel recoiled at what Jenvilno had done to Lord Belenos. His face twitched, his eye trying to focus. It rested on her and she saw with horror that the mutilated mouth above it was trying to smile. Swollen lips peeled back from broken teeth.

"Amiel," Belenos croaked. "Be careful... don't put too much faith in myths."

Blood trickled from Belenos' nose, pooled in his eye socket and drowned his eye. A lazy thread of crimson dripped from one ear, thick and dark. His final words dropped to a whisper.

"Especially the true ones."

Belenos fell silent. For nearly a minute, Jenvilno merely held him by the throat, looking down at the lord's still form on the barrier. Finally, the masked man released his grip. Amiel saw the terrible bruises Jenvilno's fingers had left on the lord's throat as his huge body slid to one side and collapsed to the ground, smearing the barrier with blood. All was silent around them. She could not even hear the breath of the crowd. Jenvilno still stared down at Belenos, and the crowd stared at Jenvilno. Finally, he nudged Belenos in the ribs with one boot.

"Get up," he ordered. His voice was even quieter now.

Belenos didn't move. Jenvilno nudged him again, harder.

"Get up. We're not done."

The boot came again, almost a kick. His voice didn't change.

"It's not over."

Movement from across the arena caught Amiel's eye. Jenvilno sensed it too, and turned as eight of Belenos' men moved toward him, armoured and with swords at their sides. Jenvilno's hands slowly clenched, he took his fighting stance again.

"Next." His voice never left its monotone.

The soldiers said nothing, they didn't slow in their march. Jenvilno didn't take his eyes off them.

"Next."

The soldiers parted as they reached him, two groups of four walking past him on either side. Jenvilno slowly followed them with his gaze, watched as they went to the crumpled remains of Belenos. The eight men laid him out on the ground, and then lifted his huge body high over their shoulders. Together, they carried their dead lord from the arena.

Chapter Thirty-Six

They left the palace silent, the court in mourning.

Amiel led the other two through the bare corridors, hunting for an exit. No one tried to stop them, but no one helped them or spoke to them either. When they passed a courtier or a soldier, they would merely hide their face and hurry past, not even daring to look at the warrior who had murdered their lord.

As they passed the door to the great throne room where they had first met Belenos, Amiel glanced through to see a huge crowd gathered. At their centre was the body of the lord, laid out on a marble slab with reverence. Around him, the people bowed their heads and stood in silence. Amiel slowed in her walking. Belenos had been dressed in his armour, and a white cloth draped over his face to conceal the worst injuries Jenvilno had inflicted on him. None of the mourners looked up as they passed the door, but as Amiel watched they closed ranks around the body of their lord, shielding it from her view. She turned her eyes ahead once more and kept walking.

Eventually, they came to a great door at the back of the palace, flanked by huge columns. To their right, the river flowed, its waters sparkling in the sun. Waiting for them was another boat. Not tied up like the others, this one had been hauled up and left on the bank, at the top of a muddy slope leading down into the clear water. It was fashioned from pale wood, almost ivory-coloured. Long and thin, it was smaller than the one they had acquired at Gwydion's gate, and like their first, had no sail.

Axel laid his shoulder to it and tried to push it down into the water, but he couldn't move it. With a gentle hand on his arm, Amiel moved him aside and began to push it herself. She feared the weight of the boat would be too much for her as well, but at the last second, as she strained with almost her entire strength, she felt it shift. The boat thundered down the slope in the silence of the meadow. Without a word, Jenvilno stepped in and took up his position at the prow. As the current pulled at it, the effect almost instant, Amiel and Axel too leapt aboard. Amiel grabbed two gnarled oars where they lay and began to row. Despite the calm surface, the current was stronger still than it had been after the Priest's church, pulling them along toward the next gate with minimal effort from her.

Sitting at the stern of the small boat, Axel looked at the masked man for a long, long time, saying nothing.

As the hours passed, and the sun began to fade, he finally spoke, his voice soft in Amiel's ear.

"It's not happening right, is it?"

Amiel looked at him sharply as she rowed, but she saw no mocking grin, none of Axel's former malice. His face was solemn as he stared at their silent ally. Amiel's own voice was quiet as she responded.

"But... he won. We got through, didn't we?"

"Yes," Axel conceded. "But Belenos was no savage." He didn't take his eyes off the masked man. "*He* was the savage. I think something is happening, Amiel, but not the way it's supposed to. I wasn't sure before, but now I think everything is going wrong."

"Belenos warned us about myths coming true," Amiel countered.

"He warned *you*," Axel corrected. "It is like I said in his palace, everything is getting worse and worse. I am afraid of how far it will go wrong, of what we'll find further ahead. I'm afraid for *us*."

With a swell of anxiety, Amiel realised their voices were growing louder. She shot a panicked glance over her shoulder at Jenvilno, but the masked man didn't react. Though he faced away from them, she still knew his grey eyes would be focused on something far beyond, his sinewy arms folded across his chest. He had not heard them. She turned back to Axel, her voice hushed once more.

"Janvier... Jenvilno doesn't have a choice. He *has* to get through, no matter the cost to him... or those he fights. We have to get through, and kill Decius."

"Why?" Axel demanded. "You seem so sure, but we don't even know what Decius is. We don't know if he is as evil as your story says. Why does he need to die?"

Peace returned to Amiel then, despite Axel's agitation. She stole a glance ahead again. The sun was sinking below the line of trees, haloed in its dying red light, she saw the outline of a tower, great and powerful against the sky.

"Not now, Axel." She squinted her eyes against the light, watching as they drew closer. "First, the final gate."

Axel followed her gaze. "It's... beautiful," he breathed. "Who awaits us there?"

"I don't know," Amiel told him. She felt his eyes on her, but her gaze remained on the tower.

"Nobody knows," she continued. "Every version of the story agrees on that. All we know is that the Knight will not stop here. He'll defeat whatever lurks there, and pass beyond."

Axel's hand found hers, and she gripped it tight. Together, they watched the tower.

The boat slid among the trees, approaching the final gate.

Mythmaking: Part Five

Janvier will come now to the final gate. No one knows what waits for him there.

Some say it is the queen of the gods herself, enraged that Janvier was gifted the great sword Lux and wanting it for herself.

Some say it is Janvier's own son, grown bitter in his father's shadow and wielding the twin to Lux, terrible Phos.

Others say the final general is the evil within Janvier himself. He will face down the darkest half of his soul, and it in turn will stare back.

Whatever guards the final gate, it will not stop Janvier.

Chapter Thirty-Seven

"Something's wrong."

As they drew closer to the tower, Amiel saw its majesty evaporate. Its great ramparts were crumbling, its stones choked with ivy and moss. It was falling apart. The river flowed directly beneath it, through the base of the tower. Their way was blocked by an iron grate, rotted with rust and strangled with more weeds. Jenvilno sprung into life and leapt into the shallow water. On the left bank were the remains of a small jetty, cracked and overgrown. Amiel threw the masked man a rope from the boat, and he tied it in three swift movements.

Their craft secured, Amiel and Axel joined the warrior on the bank. Amiel looked up, craning her neck. The tower disappeared upward, into the darkening sky. Before her, nine stone steps led up to a thick patch of creeping plants, brown and lifeless now. She climbed upward, one slow step at a time, and gripped the dry stalks in her hands. With the crunching of long-dead growth, she tore the shroud of vegetation aside to reveal an ancient door.

"How long...?" From the bottom of the steps, Axel was watching her. "How long since anyone passed through here?"

Amiel didn't answer. She didn't know. She grasped the metal handle of the door and, straining against decades of neglect, she managed to turn it and lever the door open. Trembling, Amiel stepped into a round room, which filled the entire lower floor of the tower. The river flowed through the room, from the rusted grate blocking their way to another at the opposite side. The sound of the water was all that disturbed the air. The only light struggled through the two grates and the newly opened door, barely illuminating the room. The air smelled of ancient decay, damp in Amiel's nostrils. Behind her, Axel and Jenvilno joined her in the final gateway.

They searched, and they waited. They waited for the final general of Decius to appear.

There was nothing, only silence.

"Where is the general?" Amiel asked, suddenly unsure. "Who is here?"

"It's empty." Axel's gentle voice from behind her, his hand resting on her shoulder. "No one is here."

At the edge of the stone channel where the river flowed, a metal mechanism rested on a small pedestal. Two chains ran from it to the grates at either end of the room. A huge wheel was mounted on the side of the mechanism, its spokes wider than the reach of Amiel's arms. The device was in better condition than the grates themselves, but still spotted with rust. Jenvilno strode over to it and took the spokes of the wheel in his hands. His muscles tensed as he strained, and at first Amiel thought the mechanism was useless, too rusted. She was almost certain they would go no further down this route when suddenly the wheel jerked in the masked man's hands. Inch by agonizing inch, it began to turn. The grates didn't yet move.

Amiel turned, and for the first time saw a staircase nestled against the wall, next to the door they had entered through. Cut into the inside of the tower itself, the stone steps spiralled upward into the blackness above. Her mouth set in a grim line, Amiel approached the stairs. She heard Axel's voice behind her, imploring her to wait, but she didn't slow. The youth hurried after her and, leaving Jenvilno to grapple with the huge mechanism, they began to climb the tower.

The stones were worn smooth, and mercifully in better repair than the rest of the tower. But there were enough cracks in the structure underfoot to make Amiel tread carefully. Behind her, the sound of Axel's breathing suggested he felt the same, but had more trouble hiding it. Amiel avoided looking down as they climbed higher, still remembering her near-fall on the way to Belenos. To her right, the interior of the tower yawned, and from far below she heard the wheel creak as Jenvilno turned it. The sound of the gears grew fainter as they climbed upward. It was barely audible when, finally, they reached the top of the staircase.

At first Amiel saw only the bare stone of the wall ahead of her. Then she looked up and saw, set in the ceiling, a trapdoor. Bracing her hands against it, she pushed. With a grinding of old hinges, it swung upward and she heard it clatter on the floor above her. Amiel leapt upward, her arms dragging her body through the opening. She turned, and helped Axel up after her, and they stood in the room at the top of the tower.

Four windows looked out: north, south, east and west. Amiel could see the sky above, still red with the sunset, and the canopy of the mist-wrapped forest far below them, stretching out into the twilight. The room was completely bare, and as deserted as the rest of the gatehouse. Amiel let out a long breath. She wondered if there had ever been a general at this broken gate.

"Amiel, look at this."

Axel was over by one wall, between two of the windows. She followed him over and saw that unlike the rest of the tower, the wall was not bare stone but smooth and once white, though now discoloured with age. Painted onto the wall was a mural. It was cracked and faded and covered with dirt but Amiel and Axel both reached forward and began to wipe the wall clean. Gradually, with their combined efforts, the full picture was revealed.

The art was simplistic, inexpert and almost primal. It looked like the images Amiel had seen in the oldest surviving religious texts, far from the beautiful, sinister stained glass of the Hanging Priest's church. The scene before them showed a towering figure in white. The figure's stance was majestic, powerful, and around his head a golden halo glowed. In his hand he held a shining sword.

"Is that...?" Axel faltered.

"Belenos," Amiel finished. As she spoke it, the resemblance became obvious, undeniable. Belenos stood ready for battle. He faced a terrible creature, hunched and feral. Its hands ended in claws and its body was nothing but a smear of shadow against the white stone. Its face was different, a blank disc of faded silver.

"Jenvilno," Axel breathed, reaching out to touch the twisted form.

The savage and the golden man faced one another, and Amiel saw with sadness that in the mural, the face of Belenos was calm and smiling. She looked again at the rendering of Jenvilno, but looked away quickly. She turned a slow circle in the room, her eyes raking the walls.

"Are there more?" She asked, but before Axel could answer, she was walking. She went to the left of the first mural, between the next set of windows. Again, she and Axel rubbed the dirt from the walls until the scene was revealed to them. Emerging from the filth, a bearded man in silver robes adorned this wall, and in his hand, he held a noose. The Priest. Again, this figure faced the same adversary, the twisted beast. In one claw it now held a bright blade, the same silver as its empty face. It stood more upright than in the mural where it faced the golden man. The Priest was defiant, pointing an angry finger of judgement at the animal before him. Amiel reached out a hand and touched the figure.

"Who painted these?" Axel demanded, the anger in his voice almost masking his confusion, his fear. "How did they know?"

"The same way I did," Amiel answered, not looking away from the Priest.

"But-" Axel stammered out the word. Amiel wasn't

listening. She moved to the left again, past another window, bathed in red light. Axel fell quiet once more, and together they revealed the third mural. A red-headed figure greeted them. But he didn't grin, he didn't sit at his table, boasting and joking. The painted Gwydion lay in a bed, injured. His face was turned out to the viewer and his expression was locked in a scream, terrified. Over him, the same shadowy figure crouched. It held its sword two-handed, ready to plunge downward into the wounded lord.

"But that's..." Amiel couldn't find the words this time. She resisted at first, but the other two paintings showed real scenes, though in distorted forms. She thought again of the proclamation from the barracks, of Lord Gwydion dead from injuries which hadn't been severe. "Jenvilno... he murdered Gwydion." As she voiced the thought, she knew it was true.

Axel's face was pale. "There's one wall left," he said.

Together, they walked to the final wall. Together, they reached out their hands, but at the same time they hesitated. Amiel looked into Axel's eyes. Was he as afraid as she was? Afraid of what they might see? She didn't know she was reaching for the wall until she felt the dust whisper against her fingertips, slide under the nails. Together, they drew aside the veil. All the walls were uncovered now, the circle around them complete.

The final mural, though now they knew it was the first chronologically, showed the hulking figure of a giant. His colossal body should have radiated power, even as a mere painting, but it only looked pathetic as the giant knelt and begged the shadow-creature for his life. Stained with blood from wounds all over his body, the figure of Jotun cried out for mercy in vain. Though still half-crouched, bestial, the shadow loomed over the fallen figure of the giant. Bloody sword in hand, preparing for the final strike, it looked more human than the later depictions of their journey.

Finally, it was clear to Amiel. The silent soldiers at Jotun's gate, their mysterious attack. They had wanted revenge for their lord, slaughtered by the masked monster who had been offered friendship. She remembered the silent warrior leaving the hall, his pale eyes shining. Too late she recognised that glow. It had been in his eyes when he killed the Priest, in his sword fight with Belenos.

"Amiel, the body..."

She was mystified. What was Axel talking about?

"The body," he said again. "In the river." Suddenly, she knew. She saw it again. The soldiers on the bank, watching them. The boat picking up speed in the current, and the mysterious, bloated corpse barely visible in the waters, picked at by the birds. Jotun, it had been Jotun. She looked again at the mural, the kneeling lord. He was wounded all over, but most of the cuts were to his back. She saw then what had happened. Jenvilno had chased the general out into the forest, and killed him there upon his collapse, able to run no more. But why? Why had he killed Jotun and Gwydion when they had already won their way through the gates? Looking around for further clues, she saw the final scene only when she cast her eyes upward. Her intake of breath alerted Axel, and he looked up too.

Stretching across the entire ceiling was another painting. Far more damaged by the passing time than the others, it was at first impossible to see what it depicted. The dark figure stood tall now, no longer hunched. But its face was still an eerie blank as it faced its final opponent. The painting was too degraded to see clearly, but Amiel thought she could see a figure standing ready to fight the dark man before him. She thought she saw a crown of glowing white on the second figure's head, his body marked with red, but she wasn't sure. Fear and anticipation boiled within her, and one word escaped her lips as she realised who this blurred figure must be.

"Deseme," she murmured.

It was strange. She had seen their enemy depicted before, in the church. But this crude, smeared figure haunted her. The church had shown them a lie. Decius the god. The murals around these walls depicted real events, and she knew that above her lurked an image of the true Mad King, covered in blood. She looked to Axel and, wordless, he pointed to the edge of the ceiling. Amiel saw a strange stain, far away from the two combatants.

"What is that?" she asked.

"Don't you see two more figures?"

Amiel stared, and stared, but had to admit defeat.

"No," she told him. "I see only a stain at the edge of the painting. There's nothing there."

Axel said nothing for a moment. He looked around the room again, at the black creature in its multiple forms.

"We're getting too close to him."

"He will keep us safe," Amiel reassured him, "he is the saint. I know it's changing from what I said, but-"

"*No*," Axel snapped. "He killed Jotun. He killed Gwydion. He beat Belenos to death. He is a monster, Amiel. Not a saint. If we don't walk away now, we could die too."

"It's the story of the Noble Knight and the Mad King," she countered. "Not of us. We don't matter. All we can do is help Janvier. You say he is a monster? Decius is worse. Look at his image on the ceiling, covered in blood. You heard Belenos. We have to kill him."

"Are you still so dedicated to your mission?" Axel asked. "Dedicated to orders you were given for not murdering children?"

Amiel faltered. She didn't want to admit that, at first, she had not known what he was talking about. But vaguely she remembered. The man in the distant city.

The blurred face of the woman who sent her into the forest. It wasn't important.

At that moment, a metallic shriek echoed up the tower, the sound of ancient gears grinding together.

"The grates," Amiel said. "They're opening, finally."

With a final look at the mural above, she returned to the trapdoor.

"Let's go," she ordered Axel, not waiting to see if he followed.

Jenvilno awaited them at the bottom of the tower. If turning the great wheel mechanism had tired him, the masked man didn't show it. His breathing was soft and regular, and he stood tall. As Amiel and Axel came down the stairs and walked over to him, the grey eyes behind the mask fixed on Amiel's. The gaze of the saint gripped her soul.

"Come on," he told her. He walked back to the entrance, followed by her and Axel. They walked back down the nine steps, and returned to the outside world. The sun was lower now, almost gone. Amiel could see the moon in the darkening purple of the sky. The three travellers returned to their boat and boarded. When all three were sitting in it, Jenvilno drew his sword and slashed the rope holding them in place. The current was a little faster now, and it carried the boat through the tower and out into the lands beyond. There was no need for anyone to row. Jenvilno took his position at the prow of the boat, and the other two sat. He remained standing, always in balance despite the rocking of the boat in the water. His arms were folded in front of him. Belted at his waist again, his sword lay in its sheath. Sitting at the stern, Amiel and Axel watched the man in the mask. Amiel felt Axel beside her, tense. She was calm, however. She settled back in the boat and watched their surroundings drift past them as they travelled down the river.

Chapter Twenty-Nine

Chapter Thirty-Eight

But how did you get here? What brought you to this point?

The question startled her. Not just its sudden, unwanted presence in her mind. The answer was obvious, wasn't it? She was on a mission, as Axel had said. She had disobeyed... some orders. It must have been a long time ago. It was hard to remember. She had been sent here by the grey-haired woman. Her former commander, whose name was lost now to Amiel. They had met in the besieged town. It was all so hazy. Everything before the forest. It seemed strange to the soldier, but somehow unimportant. Beneath her notice. In contrast, her childhood shone in her mind, bright and painful. Far closer to the surface than she ever allowed it.

Against her will, Amiel followed the path, so far in the past, that had brought her to this moment. The path that had brought her to the side of the saint.

You were here. You were involved. The commander's words echoed back from that distant time before the forest. The last uprising in her town against the Law of *Theos.* She had been right. Amiel had been involved. But not as a soldier. Ten years ago, she had been too young to enlist. Too young to fight. Too young to do anything except watch when the insurgents broke into her house and slaughtered her parents. Two men and a woman. The moment was seared into her memory. It still visited her late at night when she slept. When her defences were down and she couldn't force it away. She remembered every detail, except for their faces and voices. She remembered their words. She remembered their anger. But their voices had swelled in her mind to buzzing, snarling fury. Their faces were gone, leaving terrifying, nightmare figures where there had been only angry people, seeking their own bloody justice.

Amiel's parents had both been soldiers too. Highly decorated, venerated by the army of *Theos*. But for every soldier who loved them, who saluted their medals, there were three angry sons and daughters of the frontiers. Men and women who had lost parents and grandparents under the banner of *Theos*. When the uprising sparked into terrible life, they were among the first targets.

Amiel remembered the first hammering at the door. The smell of smoke from outside. Her mother telling her to run upstairs and hide while her father took out their armour and weapons from the chest they had been consigned to years before. They had time only to take up their swords when the doors burst inward and Amiel's life as it was ended. The enraged words of the rebels. The defiance of her parents. The end and the beginning.

The soldiers of *Theos* rallied. Superior arms and discipline crushed the greater numbers and righteous anger of the conquered. They were conquered again. Curfews and increased military presence at first, strict enforcement. Then local leaders were courted, soldiers intermingled with the townsfolk again. Ringleaders or scapegoats were put forward for execution. An uneasy peace returned, which would become more natural over the years.

A good try. A failed rebellion. You had your chance. Now we are all friends again. Obey the laws of *Theos*, and be quiet. And the only cost was the lives of those who died. And those like Amiel of course, left behind.

Cleaning up in the aftermath of that first riot, they found her in a cupboard upstairs. Tears dried on her face. A dagger in her small hands. Two soldiers with friendly voices and shining faces brought her to the barracks with the other children who had lost their parents. They took the dagger first. She didn't like that. She felt naked.

Defenceless, she went into the first orphanage. So began her tour of the villages around her hometown. One orphanage to the next. Some kind, some cruel. Most just full to bursting point with the children of the war, from both sides. A marching line of angry adults and angry children. The children, of course, divided themselves along the lines of the war, wounds still bleeding. Your father was a traitor. Your mother was *Theos* scum. The price of victory was that the children of the dead rebels now outnumbered Amiel and the other orphans of the *Theos* Empire.

There, she had learned to fight. She had learned to win at all costs. But every victory was hollow. Every fight won ended the same. Dragged to the cold offices of the masters, blood still on her fists. There, she would be beaten. Beaten in the name of *Theos*. The violence and sin beaten from her. She had learned that *Theos* was an uncaring god, distant and neglectful. The god of beatings and cruelty. The god of adults making no attempt to understand her. In search of a wider meaning to her life, she had dismissed the god who wanted nothing to do with her.

A year into her sentence of five. She began to read. Already interested in religion and history by that point, she had found an even deeper fascination, a need, within herself. It was at the third orphanage, reading their meagre library, that she had rediscovered the name of Janvier. Worshipped in the area, the name to her had, up until then, meant dull trips to the church on festival days before the rebellion. Momentary distraction by the glass and lily-adorned statue, before boredom reclaimed her. Not so now.

Here was a saint who, unlike his god, cared for her. He cared for soldiers. For those who would help themselves. For those who would protect the weak against evil. She read every book she could find on him. Read them multiple times. There were still fights, and there were still beatings. But she no longer fought for her own pride. She no longer fought in anger. Janvier wanted her to fight only for those who couldn't. Janvier fought for justice, not hatred. From the moment she read his name in that orphanage library, Amiel swore that she would be a soldier like him. She swore that she would stop children from suffering like she did.

Four years later, she left the orphanage old enough to join the army. She enlisted that same day.

Forged in hundreds of fights over those five years, she excelled in training. Reading had honed her natural intelligence. It was a fast path upwards, and the tenth squadron had been the obvious choice. Dirty wars against rebels, against the kind of people who had killed her parents. She was doing the work of Janvier.

Until that final mission. The children behind the wall hanging. Her refusal to kill them. She remembered that. She looked back now without regret. She knew why she had disobeyed. She had sworn not to let children suffer. She had sworn to protect the weak. She had disobeyed her orders because it was what the saint wanted. It had been a test of her resolve, and she had passed. And he had used it to call her to his side, to bring her to the forest. He had summoned her to help him destroy Deseme.

The boat drifted on.

Chapter Thirty-Nine

First, the trees lining their way died. Patches of dark, dead leaves began to appear. These grew larger and larger, until all around them, no living leaves clung to any branches. As the hours passed and the uneasy sun began to disappear altogether, the surface of the water ahead grew choked with fallen leaves. Amiel leaned over the side of the boat and trailed her hand in the water, grasping at some of the leaves floating on the surface. The waters numbed her hand almost instantly, and quickly she grabbed a leaf and withdrew her arm. Examining her catch, she saw that she held ash leaves. She looked to the trees along the bank once more. They were bare at this point in the river, their pointed branches jutting upward and outward. But soon those skeletal trunks were gone too, replaced by stumps struggling from overgrown grass. Finally, even these remnants of the trees fell away, and on either side of the river there was only grass, a vast meadow in the dark. Far, far away Amiel thought she could see the tree line, not gone, only receded. But it could have just been greater shadow in the distance, and she was far from sure.

The grass in the meadow died next, and they sailed through a true wasteland, spotted here and there with ancient, carved blocks of stone. Unfamiliar architecture from a city long gone to the earth. Then, all at once, the flowers appeared. Amiel didn't need to look closer to know what they were, but she did in respect to the saint with her.

Lily of the Valley. Impossibly numerous, the flowers filled each bank with glowing white, the dead land around the travellers reborn. Blooms floated in the water ahead and around them, as if strewn by supplicants.

The river began to widen. Ahead of them, something was emerging from the darkness. Amiel's breath caught, and a small sound of awe escaped her mouth as a structure shrugged off its cloak of shade and began to take shape, glorious and terrible.

Rising from the great river, widening now to a huge lake in the expanse of the flower meadow, Amiel saw their destination.

At first, she saw it as a great fortress, the stronghold of a king or a warlord. Its fortifications were grim and foreboding, turrets rising in predatory spikes, walls sprouting straight from the dark waters, crowned with mighty battlements. As they grew closer, however, it took on the shape of a vast cathedral. Where before she had seen defences, she now looked upon a monument to a god. The only god. On the breath of the wind, she almost thought she heard the tolling of a bell, the sound mournful. Closer still, and now she could not tell what it was they were sailing toward. It could have been a castle, or a place of worship. A palace or a prison. It speared into the sky, vertically from the lake, its stones shining in the moonlight.

"Amiel... it's almost over, isn't it?" Axel's voice beside her, all doubt crushed from it, caught between terror and awe. "Whatever is happening, we're reaching the end."

Amiel nodded. A strange feeling at her mouth, and she realised she was smiling. She tilted her head back, her face illuminated by the silver of the moon, and she couldn't stop smiling. Her heart was peaceful within her.

"Yes," she agreed, the words feeling warm in her chest; feeling right. "Yes, Axel. This is where it ends."

She felt a hand at her shoulder, and she slowly turned to look at the youth.

"We don't have to go on," he said. "You know that, don't you? We could stop now. We could turn away. We don't have to go in there."

"Yes, I do." Her refusal was gentle, still she smiled. "I have to see."

Axel nodded, as if he had expected no other answer. When he spoke, his voice was heavy with resignation.

"Why? Why did he sail all this way? Why does he have to kill Decius?"

Amiel's gaze was drawn back to their destination.

"To rescue his bride," she answered at last. "The bride Deseme took from him."

"Amiel-" Axel couldn't go on. It would have been useless anyway.

"The Mad King took Janvier's bride," Amiel told him. "He took her to his citadel, and there he waited. Janvier fought hard, he triumphed at every one of the gates, against every one of the generals. Noble, he stood against them, and never lost sight of his mission. He is ready now to fight Deseme. To rescue his Bride, wounded by the Mad King. We cannot turn back. She needs us."

Amiel stood up now, stepped further forward in the boat. She stared unblinking into the moonlight as they finally reached the House of Deseme.

Mythmaking: The End

At last, Janvier will reach the throne room of the Mad King. Deseme will await him there with his prisoner, the knight's beautiful Bride. Deseme took her from noble Janvier, envying their love, and the knight swore that he would hide his face behind his helm until he had brought her safely home.

He will stand before Deseme, and demand the return of his love. The Mad King will only laugh, and leap to attack his hated enemy. Drawing Lux for the final time, Janvier will go to battle.

For three days and nights they will fight, neither able to best the other's strength. Janvier is powerful, his cause just, his blade tested against terrible enemies at every gate. But Deseme is strong too, his sword fast, his body given speed and power by his madness.

On and on they will fight, until finally the evil Deseme, knowing he can never conquer the might of Janvier, will attack the knight's Bride where she stands, leaving her with a terrible wound. Janvier will run to aid her, but Deseme will now attack with a new fury. Within Janvier, rage will begin to burn. He will raise shining Lux high, and strike Deseme down, mortally injuring the Mad King. In his final moments, the evil Deseme will try to take Janvier with him into death, but after nine steps, he will fall.

Janvier will rush to the side of the woman he loves. She will still live, but her wound will be severe and her blood will stain the floor of the throne-room.

Tenderly, the noble knight will pick her up, and carry her back to the boat.

Together, they will sail away, the Mad King dead in his hall.

Chapter Forty

The boat drifted toward the castle. Its drawbridge was down, the end resting on a smaller sandbank in the centre of the river, providing a place for their boat to land. They drifted to a gentle stop on partially-submerged sand, and Jenvilno was the first out of the boat. He didn't stop to tie it up, and Amiel followed him as the masked man stepped onto the bridge. Axel walked beside her, but Amiel looked only ahead, toward the colossal stone arch marking the entrance to Deseme's fortress.

"Will she survive?" The words didn't register at first, she only kept walking.

"Will the bride survive her wound?" Axel asked again.

For a moment, Amiel's steps faltered. She stopped, and turned to the boy. She placed a hand on his shoulder.

"What do you think, Axel?" She asked. She stepped closer, her hand leaving his shoulder as she slid her arm around his neck. Axel jerked, surprised, but then returned the embrace. Amiel smiled against his neck. The man she thought of as a youth, who was her own age.

"This has been a trial," she said. "But I am glad you were here with me."

The kiss she left on his lips bore no desire. It wasn't love, but a blessing. The enactment of a rite. She stepped away from him. Axel said nothing, but when she walked after Jenvilno, he followed. Their feet rang hollow on the wood of the drawbridge until they finally reached the great stone arch.

Passing through the gateway, Amiel felt a chill settle on her skin as they found themselves in a courtyard within the outer walls of the fortress. Soft, icy breezes slid between the stones and whispered around the three of them as they walked on, silent.

It was deserted. Where were the soldiers of the Mad King? The ragged army of the bandit lord? The followers of the burning god? Amiel saw no one, heard nothing. The only sound was the hiss of the river as it flowed around the castle's tiny island.

It didn't matter. Ahead of them was the keep, grim and still, in the centre of the courtyard. Crimson banners hung from its walls, and its spires rose high into the dark sky above. In the wall facing them was a doorway. The doors stood closed, but still seemed to beckon the travellers. Amiel saw the end of her journey. She saw the fulfilment of her faith. She strode toward the door, but a dark form overtook her.

Jenvilno's strides were longer, his step quicker. His footsteps made no sound as he walked to the door and set his hands against it. His feet planted wide apart, he bowed his head slightly, and Amiel heard a sigh, almost lost in the sound of the river, from his hidden mouth. His arms tensed against the doors, and in one movement, he pushed them open. They swung inward, revealing a blackness deeper than the night around them. Without a pause, Jenvilno walked through and vanished. Amiel walked in next, leaving Axel outside to follow.

The three stepped out of the wind, into a cramped stone corridor. Torches burned on the walls, held in brackets of gold. Crimson hangings decorated the walls. They walked in single file, the corridor too small for anything else. The ceiling was low, forcing Jenvilno to duck as they walked. It stretched on so far, deeper even than the god-mountains they had entered so long ago. There was total silence now. None of them spoke, even their breathing made no sound. They only moved forward, toward whatever awaited them. Amiel thought of her journey. She thought of everything she had gone through. The deviations from the truth she knew. The tests she had braved. The terrible blows to her faith, and its ultimate survival. Still she felt at peace. She knew now what they were here for, who they were here to save.

At last, the corridor ended in another set of doors. Beyond them was the Bride, beyond them was the Mad King. It was time. Jenvilno reached out and pushed these doors open too, and walked into the cavernous room beyond. One final time, Amiel followed the saint.

Chapter Forty-One

The room was vast. The ceiling, as high as the sky itself, streamed with red silk hangings. Torch-flames flickered everywhere, stars trapped under stone, clinging to the walls. Chandeliers hung from the ceiling. Great black candlesticks, as tall as Amiel, stood in a burning forest across the floor. A path had been cleared through them, toward the front of the room, carpeted in red and gold.

Jenvilno walked down this path, light and shadow playing across his dark, dirty clothes and bare arms, his black hair and his mask. Amiel and Axel followed, silent in the oppressive atmosphere of the room. Surrounded by thousands of tiny points of flame, they approached the front of the chamber. It was a long way, and at first the far wall was out of focus. But eventually, Amiel saw that it was decorated again with hanging crimson, forming a ghostly pyramid of flowing silk against the dark stone. Six great, wide steps, stretching across the entire width of the room, greeted them. The candlesticks rose with the steps, surrounding the mighty throne on the final stair with light. Crafted of wood and gold, dark metal and crimson, the seat stood majestic at the very centre of the back wall. Flanked on either side with two great urns of shining, crystalline glass, the throne was empty.

"Decius."

The sudden noise startled Amiel. It burst from the mouth of Jenvilno, far louder than anything she had heard from him before. His voice rose to a shout, to a roar.

"Decius."

For an insane moment, it sounded to her like he was smiling, behind the mask.

"DECIUS!"

The masked man's war cry tore through the throne-room, disturbing the crimson hangings and causing the flames to dance around them.

As the noise died away, the laughter began. It was a horrifying sound, cracked and musical. Amiel heard fury in that howling, and terrible joy. It came from behind them. As one, the three travellers turned to its source.

Decius, the great enemy, the man who had once attacked a village in another life; the man she had entered the forest to kill, stood behind them, in the path between the candles. Amiel's eyes narrowed and her hand went to her sword as she finally looked upon the Mad King.

He was tall, and his build slender, like Jenvilno. He was clad in a full suit of silver armour, which glittered as he bathed in the light of the candles. His hair was white, and Amiel thought of the figure from the murals at the final gate, its head crowned with snow. Decius' hair was sleek and soft, falling to his armoured shoulders and half-hiding his face. An armoured fist delicately brushed a strand away from his eyes as he grinned at them. The eyes which glared from his face were ice-blue, incredibly pale. They slid in and out of focus, from serenity to fury, as he regarded his guests. The laughter stopped seeping from near-colourless lips, and the Mad King walked toward them. Still, he smiled.

Axel froze with terror beside her, but Amiel barely noticed. The presence of Decius, his *existence*, sent her body screaming into revolt. He moved differently, like Jenvilno. But where the saint walked and fought with the mark of the divine, the movements of Decius were *wrong*, and disgusted her. His face was beautiful, but something about it was too intense, almost less than human. Her heart raced, and her skin felt cold as he approached. She tensed, ready for battle.

But Jenvilno didn't move. He remained motionless

as Decius strolled past all three of them and ascended the steps to his throne. The chamber was silent as he turned and sat, his elbows resting on his knees, arms loosely folded. Still he stared at them with the direct, unblinking gaze of a child or a madman. Finally, Decius spoke, and his voice was clear and calm.

"Jenvilno." He smiled down at the masked man. "You've come, at last."

Even if the masked man was going to reply, Amiel spoke first.

"Decius," she said, her voice strong, filling the room. "We have come to kill you."

She felt the full force of his gaze on her now, an almost physical pressure. Though it made her tremble, she set her jaw and stared back at him. Failing to stare her down, or else losing interest, he spoke.

"Kill me?" still he smiled, his voice almost warm. "You can't even comprehend me."

Amiel faltered, but recovered enough to speak.

"You *will* die here," she repeated. "We have fought our way through all of your gates. We have defeated all of your generals. We have entered your House undefeated."

Decius leaned forward a little closer. He tilted his head to one side, and now genuine curiosity slipped into his words, as if every time he spoke, he was a different person.

"And that means you'll defeat me too?" he asked. "You think I'm like the others? You think I'm just a zealot with a rope? A slimy trickster with a quick tongue? I'm *Decius*!"

Without warning, he sat upright as he hissed his name. His fist struck against his chest with a ring of metal against metal. The sound slowly died away, and no one spoke. Decius' head swivelled again to regard her, a reptilian movement. Amiel shuddered.

"You belong in hell." The words were venomous, full

of malice. She only realised she had spoken them afterwards.

"I tried to go there," he answered her. "They barred the gates and hid."

Decius ignored her now, and spoke again to Jenvilno.

"It *is* good to see you again, Jenvilno." There was malicious humour in his voice now, though Jenvilno merely stared back, unmoving. "Do you remember the last time we met? Do you remember how we fought then?"

He leant a little further forward, his voice darkening. "Do you remember the scars?"

Jenvilno's hand rose to the lower half of his mask, where his mouth was hidden beneath the metal.

"How could I forget?" his voice was barely more than a sigh.

Amiel began to step forward, felt Axel try to hold her back. She shrugged him off and spoke once more to Decius.

"What are you?" she asked him. "At every gate, we heard something new. What are you? Why do you speak to him like you know him?"

Decius chuckled.

"I am the son of Jenvilno, and his father. I am his closest former friend, and his most hated enemy. I am the Eternal Adversary, I am the Constant Opposite."

His smile shone on her once more.

"I am Decius."

"We heard you were a king," Amiel persisted. "A bandit lord. We heard you were a god."

Decius was shaking his head. He indicated Jenvilno with an armoured hand, a casual gesture.

"No, no. I am the devil, and he is the god," he told her. "Though sometimes we change places."

Amiel was mystified. Nothing was making sense. She shook her head to clear it of Decius's words. He was a madman. It was pointless to seek sense in what he said. She looked now around the room, noticing something for the first time. Her hand began to ease her sword free as she asked her new question.

"Where is the Bride?" she demanded.

Decius' face was blank.

"Excuse me?" he asked, a smile returning to his face.

"We sailed here, through your gates, to find Jenvilno's Bride," she told him. "You took her, hating them. Envying their love. Where is she?"

Decius shook his head slowly, the soft sound of mirth in his throat. He rested his face gently in one hand as he laughed. Recovering himself, his blue eyes found Amiel after a moment's searching.

"That's what you heard, is it?" She saw pity in his smile for a second and hated it. "I am afraid it is not true."

He looked at her still, but really, he spoke to Jenvilno.

"No, it's not lost love our masked friend fights for. It's not justice, or to rid the world of my evil. Nothing noble brought my friend here."

He shifted focus to the masked man, addressing him directly now.

"No. I know what you want. I can see it now. A tower of corpses, piled as high as the sky itself. A monument to a life finally ended. Buried beneath a tomb of fallen opponents. And at the top of it all, an epitaph reading 'In Honour of the Strongest'. Isn't that right, *Jenvilno*?"

Decius spat the name of the masked warrior, suddenly furious. Beside her, Amiel felt Jenvilno trembling. His hand went to his waist, and over his ragged breathing, the scraping sound of his sword leaving its sheath was thunderous. She looked at the blade. It glowed brighter than it ever had, its light otherworldly. Its shape seemed to shimmer. Now serrated, now curved, now long, now a shortsword again. She blinked, and the shimmering vanished.

"*Lux,*" she breathed. How could she ever have doubted?

Twin scabbards hung at Decius's waist. He reached slowly down and slid two short, curved blades from them. His elbows resting on his knees, one hand dangling downward between them, he tapped the point of that blade against his armoured shin as he leaned forward, his grin widening.

"Is it time again already, Jenvilno? Do you think it will be any different tonight?"

He stood now, took three steps forward. He stopped at the very edge of the top step, looking down at Jenvilno alone.

"I don't care." He answered his own questions. His grin was impossibly wide. "Come on now. It's the end."

Decius descended the stairs, and Jenvilno's hand tensed around his blade. Somewhere far away, Amiel wondered if this was the first time Jenvilno had sailed up the river. Her distracted thoughts vanished as the final battle began.

Chapter Forty-Two

Jenvilno charged forward, half-hunched. Decius hurled himself from the stairs with a screaming laugh. They clashed together, and Decius slammed a kick into Jenvilno's body. The masked man stumbled, knocking over a cluster of the heavy black candlesticks. Amiel tensed as they fell, still burning, but the floor around them was bare stone and the flames did nothing but gutter out and fade into darkness. Jenvilno slipped to his knees, but blocked a following blow from Decius's twin blades and forced his way to his feet. Jenvilno launched three murderous cuts at Decius, but the man in the armour only laughed and danced around them, sending back vicious strikes of his own. Amiel was stunned. Decius fought with ten times the Priest's fury, with the cunning Gwydion wished he had, with skill Belenos could never hope to match. At last she understood one thing Decius had said, sat in his throne. She couldn't kill him, she couldn't comprehend swordplay, speed and power so great.

She could only watch Jenvilno, their one hope of defeating the Mad King, as he fought for their lives. She didn't care what Decius said about the Bride. She knew he was lying. Everything else had been right. She was here somewhere.

Decius never stopped talking. As he fought Jenvilno, madness trickled from his lips. Amiel didn't know whether it was a deliberate tactic to disrupt Jenvilno's concentration, or if Decius merely couldn't help himself. Whichever it was, she feared Decius was distracting even Jenvilno with his words.

"High! Low! Left! Left! Right! Low!" Decius called as he attacked, the words not relating at all to his true movements. Jenvilno parried and deflected, but found no room to launch an attack of his own.

"You are *slow*," Decius snarled around his smile. "*Weak*. But was this ever about strength? Was it ever decided on speed?" He feinted left, attacked to the right. Jenvilno didn't dodge quickly enough, and one of Decius's blades raked down his side. It sliced through the thin material of Jenvilno's jacket and blood began to well immediately from the wound, black in the candlelight.

"Blood brothers again!" Decius screamed. Jenvilno blocked another attack, and a ferocious cut of his own screeched down Decius's breastplate.

Fire flared within Amiel. Her fists clenched in anticipation. Decius only grinned.

The man with white hair looked down at his armour. *Lux* had torn a wide gash into the front, snaking down from Decius's left shoulder to his stomach. Decius looked at it, and then back to his opponent.

"Well, I suppose this makes things a little fairer," he shrugged. With a sudden cry of joy, he plunged his armoured fingers into the tear and dragged it open. Amiel felt terror at Decius' strength as he easily ripped his breastplate away and threw it in pieces to the floor. Sheathing his blades momentarily, he threw aside the gauntlets and the arm guards as well. Naked now from the waist up, a crimson sash trailed to his mid-shin, freed from his armour. He was dressed exactly as the white-haired figure was from the stained-glass windows in the church, so far behind them now. Seeing Amiel watching him, he mockingly stretched out his arms, his feet together, mirroring the pose of the god. She saw ligature marks at his neck she would have sworn were not there before. She recoiled, and with a grin he turned back to Jenvilno, drawing his blades once more.

Idly, Decius twirled one through his fingers, one eye on the masked man. Without warning, he attacked once more. He slashed right and left with his twin blades, pushing Jenvilno back. Together, they tore through the throne room, smashing candlesticks wherever they went. Gradually, the room slipped into an uneasy twilight as more and more of the candles fell and guttered out. Jenvilno again was on the defensive, trying and failing to find an opening to attack Decius. The Mad King let him lunge forward once, but sliced a cut into Jenvilno's shoulder. As before with Belenos, Amiel saw Jenvilno grow angrier and angrier as he fought. Decius was playing with him, and Jenvilno couldn't match him.

Decius parried Jenvilno, knocking him off balance. As he stumbled forward, the king slammed his armoured knee up into the masked man's stomach, knocking the breath from him. Jenvilno staggered back to his feet, ready for the next attack. It never came.

Decius stood a few paces away, shaking his head,

"Underwhelming," was all he said at first. "Is this all you can do? It just seems unfair to kill someone so inferior."

He smiled now, eyes glittering.

"Perhaps," he murmured, "I should just leave you alive."

With a roar of fury, Jenvilno lunged. He raised his sword high, and brought it hammering downward at Decius's unprotected chest. Amiel's eyes blazed, certain that the Mad King was about to die. Decius didn't parry this blow, he met force with force. He raised one of his curved blades, and blocked Jenvilno's blow as it fell.

There was a terrible, metallic scream as the blades met.

Jenvilno's sword shattered.

The shining blade cracked into three pieces, and fell to the darkness of the floor. Glowing no more, the shards merely lay on the stone, worthless and pathetic.

"*Lux!*" there was despair in Amiel's words.

Decius stepped back, head tilted to one side.

"What now, Jenvilno?" he smiled. The masked man

looked at the hilt in his hand, and the two inches of jagged metal still clinging to it. He threw it to one side and slowly, his hands clenched into fists. He brought them up before his masked face, and with cold, grey eyes fixed on his opponent, he began to advance.

"*Excellent,*" Decius grinned. He gave his twin blades a glance, then threw them to the floor. He didn't raise his own fists, he only held his arms wide and grinned as Jenvilno attacked.

The masked man slammed a punch into Decius's perfect teeth. He thundered two blows into the Mad King's face, drew blood from his lips and tore his skin.

Decius only laughed. Jenvilno screamed again with rage, and beat Decius with sickening, devastating blows. But still the Mad King laughed and still words bubbled from his bloody mouth.

"I'm only Decius as long as I live!" he howled through his grin. "You must kill me, to become the new Decius!"

Jenvilno's fist fell once more, and Decius caught it.

The man with white hair shrieked laughter, and smashed his fist into Jenvilno's midsection. The warrior fell to his knees, and his opponent's armoured foot cracked against his skull and ribs. Decius kicked him again, and again. Jenvilno tried to stand, but another kick sent him staggering into the candles once more. He tripped over black metal bases and fell, candlesticks toppling all around him. This time the flames didn't die straight away, but smouldered still, surrounding the masked man with a ring of dying fire. He tried to sit up, and fell back. Blood seeped from a wound to the side of his head, and his grey eyes slid shut.

Decius watched him. Not taking his eyes from Jenvilno, the grinning man crouched low, slowly reaching for the floor. Amiel gasped as she saw him take one of his fallen blades from the stone, the razor edge rasping against the ground as he lifted it. She wanted to move, to save her Janvier, but she was paralysed as Decius took up his blade and began to creep toward where Jenvilno lay.

As Decius walked toward his victim, he passed close to her.

He stopped. With a creaking of bone, his neck moving in jerks, he turned to her. Smiling wide, blue eyes burning bright.

"We all have our parts to play." His voice was serene.

The blade flashed out and plunged into her stomach.

Chapter Forty-Three

The pain was a searing fire. It was burning cold. Decius dragged his blade back out again, tearing more flesh. Amiel clutched her stomach, tried to stop the blood, warm against her flesh as it began to spurt from her. Her killer watched her in silence. He smiled in a half-distracted way, mildly diverted.

Her legs tried to buckle, but Amiel wouldn't let them. Her vision tried to blur, but she fought it off. Her hand on his bare shoulder, she held herself up, staring into his pale eyes. Her other hand was heavy at her side, but dragging it upward, she reached for her waist. Finally, as her strength flowed from the wound, her hand closed on the object at her belt. Axel's knife. A breath escaped her tortured lungs, loud as a scream, as she drew the blade. Her other hand left his shoulder and, as she began to fall forward, caught a fistful of his hair in a death grip. Drawing herself close to the Mad King, she raised the blade high and drove it into his flesh.

It entered his shoulder, slammed deep by her weight and her dying rage. He stumbled back with a hiss, his smile faltering but not disappearing. He dislodged himself from her embrace, and staggered back. Amiel tried to take a step, but her legs were weak and she stumbled, half-turning. She fell against someone, felt herself cradled in a pair of strong arms, held up. She tried to speak, choked out blood, finally forced out the word.

"Axel?"

She looked up, into the blank metal mask. Jenvilno held her in his arms. His grey eyes looked down into hers. The pain grew, Amiel's vision blurred,

"Please..." she whispered. "Help."

Long moments stretched out. Jenvilno held her

against him, saying nothing. Then he released her, and stepped around her as she fell to the floor.

Amiel felt the stone, cool against her. She lay on her back. Her head rolled to one side, and she saw Jenvilno step again toward Decius, fists raised in his guard once more. She tried to smile. Of course. It had only ever been about those two. Everything else around them was just a minor detail, and minor details could be changed or removed with no consequence.

She felt another pair of hands on her now. Gentle, they lifted her, and now she looked up into Axel's face. His hat was gone, fallen off somewhere, and a curl of his golden hair tickled her brow as he held her. His eyes shone with tears waiting to fall, his mouth trying to speak.

With an arm weighing almost too much for her to lift, she raised her hand and touched his lips.

"No, Axel," she murmured. The pain was going away now, becoming less important. "It's too late. Maybe you were right. Maybe we got too close. Maybe we could have turned away. But now... let me see the end."

Axel nodded, his tears beginning to fall. He held her up with a gentle strength she would never have guessed was within him, and so she saw the moment when Jenvilno took off his mask.

The fighter's hands travelled slowly upward to the leather strap holding it to his face, and with fingers that shook slightly he unfastened it. With the strap clutched tightly in one fist, the mask hanging from it, Jenvilno stared at the wounded Decius. He stood almost facing Amiel where she lay, but she couldn't see his face in the half-light of the throne room. The air shimmered again, and her vision blurred further as the blood left her body. Occasionally, however, candlelight would flicker across his face, and she would glimpse him. But every time, his face was different.

She saw him as young and beautiful. She saw him with the grizzled face of a jaded soldier, covered in scars. She saw him with a white beard, older even than the Hanging Priest. She saw him as a god, as a murderer and finally as a saint. She looked upon all these faces with a smile as her eyes finally closed.

Axel held Amiel close as her breathing stopped. His body shook with grief. He squeezed his eyes shut as hard as he could, not caring if he was next to die.

Then, slowly, his eyelids opened once more, and he watched the two warriors fight. They fought on the steps before the throne. Badly wounded now, bright blood dripping from his shoulder, Decius continued to fight like a cornered animal. His stance unsteady and his movements clumsy, he still dominated Jenvilno. The other man's mask lay close to Axel, and Decius now rained fierce punches on his enemy's exposed face, fighting with his uninjured arm alone but still deadly. The Mad King laughed as another blow connected, and Jenvilno fell against the throne. He upset one of the great glass urns, and it rolled toward the white-haired man. Decius stopped it under one foot, grinned down at it.

Slowly, he raised the foot, an expression of mock care on his face.

With a cry, he plunged his foot downward, shattering the urn into shards. Decius bent down and swept up three of the glittering pieces with his good hand. Turning away from Jenvilno, he gently placed the pieces, long and jagged, between the fingers of his left hand. With a smile, he turned back to Jenvilno, his glass-filled fist held ready. His stance lowered slowly, his bloody shoulder dropped. There was nothing sane left in his face as he glared at his enemy.

"Come... on..." he snarled, agony in his voice and blood on his teeth. "Let's... end... this... again..."

For the last time, Jenvilno attacked.

Decius was ready.

Screaming his terrifying laughter, the white-haired man sliced once, twice, across Jenvilno's chest. The glass sliced deep into flesh, but not fatally. Decius punched straight with the glass now, and caught Jenvilno in the shoulder. The warrior cried in agony as the glass pierced him. Decius only laughed, even though blood dripped from his own hand where the shards had pushed back against his palm. He clenched his fist tighter, smiling as droplets of red fell from it.

"I can feel it," he murmured. "Are you ready?" He leapt, the glass-filled fist lancing forward.

Weakened by the wound Amiel had dealt him, this time the madman was not fast enough. Jenvilno caught his arm. Twisting, pulling, the warrior dragged Decius off-balance. As he stumbled, Jenvilno drove his fist three times backhand into the other man's jaw, still holding his enemy's wrist.

When Decius stumbled, Jenvilno grabbed his glass-filled fist and forced it backward. Axel wished Amiel was still alive as the shards bit deep into Decius' gut. He stumbled backward, losing his grip on the sharp glass pieces. Held in place by his torn flesh now, they jutted from his body. He nearly fell, but somehow managed to stay standing. His smile was gone, his eyes showed only rage as he began to stagger toward Jenvilno. His hands hooked into claws, he snapped and spat and bit his own lips in his frenzy.

"Kill you. *I'll kill you!* I'll-"

Decius stopped. He looked down at the blades of glass buried in his flesh. Slowly, he began to laugh again. It started off low, almost restrained. Then it began to rise, becoming a deranged howl. His head was tilted back, his eyes unfocussed as he laughed. His shoulders shook with the force of it. As it reached a demented pitch, his hands locked around the shards in his gut and he dragged them upward. He tore the wound in his stomach into crimson tatters, clawed it open. Blood soaked his armoured legs as he finally fell to the floor, before his throne.

Jenvilno stepped in close, and Axel heard Decius speak for the final time.

"Another... missed opportunity... for you... Jenvilno." Decius forced the words out, laughing softly still. His voice was barely a whisper, but Axel heard the anger and joy as he mocked the other man.

"Perhaps... someone else can give you what you want. But I don't... think so. There was... only me. In honour of the strongest... goodbye, *Jenvilno.*"

His smile growing wider still, blood at the corners of his mouth, Decius' head rolled back and his icy eyes grew dull.

Deseme was dead.

Chapter Forty-Four

It was beginning to rain as Axel walked back along the drawbridge. His footsteps rang hollow against the wood, dragging, uneven beneath the weight he carried. In his arms, he held the body of Amiel.

Her face was pale. Wrapped in his jacket, the terrible wound in her body hidden, Axel still couldn't look at her. He reached the sandbank in the river and saw, somehow, their boat was still there. Gently, he laid Amiel down in it.

A small sound behind him. He turned. Jenvilno stood watching him, the rain mingling with the blood and dirt on his clothes and skin. He wore his mask once more, and his eyes stared at Axel for the first time, not through him.

He wanted to feel angry, but he just felt weary. He wanted to force the masked killer to understand what they had gone through at his side. How much worse it had been for them, so far removed from what he was. The words were lost within him, somewhere broken and haunted. He wanted to stare back, to defy this presence in a man's skin. Instead, he dropped his eyes.

Jenvilno didn't react. He turned, and vanished back into the shadows of the castle. No footsteps in the water announced the direction he had taken, which bank he had gone to. He was merely gone. It was over, then.

Axel shook his head. No, it wasn't. He thought about myths, and how long they lasted. How many different ways they could unfold. It was never over. He wondered where Jenvilno would go next, who he would drag into his wake, and what misery he would bring them.

As he climbed into the boat himself, he tried to remember the fighter's face, but it had been dark in the throne room, and he had been too far away to see. All he could remember was a pair of grey eyes, staring out from behind a metal mask.

He took his place in the boat, Amiel's head held in his lap.

Axel pushed off and sailed away.

About the Author

Jonathan Watts was born on the 1st of October 1988 in Torquay, England.

Growing up in North Yorkshire, he was fascinated by mythology from a very early age, and went on to study Classics to MA level at Newcastle University.

Always an avid reader, at the age of 13 Jonathan picked up his first David Gemmell novel in an airport while travelling to New York. The characters, action and emotion all resonated with Jonathan in a way that no previous author had, and from then on it became his dream to be a published novelist.

Over a decade and a half of hard, frequently discouraging work followed, but Jonathan never gave up. It wasn't an option to give up. Finally, he found success with Bury Me Where They Fall – a dark, surreal book marrying his interest in folklore and mythology to a nightmarish "Apocalypse Now"-inspired narrative.

Jonathan currently resides in Bristol, where he spends his time working as a copywriter, reading and seeing every live band he can manage to see.